The
Not-Just-Anybody
Family

Also by Betsy Byars

THE NIGHT SWIMMERS
THE ANIMAL, THE VEGETABLE, AND JOHN D
   JONES

The
Not-Just-Anybody
Family

BETSY BYARS

Illustrated by Jacqueline Rogers

DELACORTE PRESS/NEW YORK

Published by
Delacorte Press
1 Dag Hammarskjold Plaza
New York, New York 10017

Text copyright © 1986 by Betsy Byars

Illustrations copyright © 1986 by Jacqueline Rogers

Manufactured in the United States of America

First printing

Library of Congress Cataloging in Publication Data
Byars, Betsy Cromer.
 The not-just-anybody family.

 Summary: With a young brother in the hospital, a
grandfather in jail, and their mother traveling with a
rodeo, Maggie and Vern try to settle family problems.
 [1. Brothers and sisters—Fiction. 2. Family
problems—Fiction] I. Rogers, Jackie, ill. II. Title.
PZ7.B98396No 1986   [Fic]
ISBN 0-385-29443-3
Library of Congress Catalogue Card Number 85-16184

For Eddie

On and off the Barn

JUNIOR STOOD ON TOP OF THE BARN, ARMS OUT-stretched, legs apart. Strapped to his thin arms were wings made out of wire, old sheets, and staples—his own design. His mouth hung open. His eyes watched a spot over the cornfield where he hoped to land. He appeared to be praying.

"Go ahead and jump," his brother, Vern, called.

"Give him time," his sister, Maggie, said. She was sitting cross-legged on the ground, painting her fingernails with a green Magic Marker.

"Well, if he doesn't jump before Pap gets home, he won't get to jump. Junior, Pap won't let you jump. If he catches you up there on the barn, he'll whup you."

Junior kept watching the small grassy clearing beyond the cornfield. He was trying to watch it long enough to make it his body's destination. He felt his body had to know where it was supposed to go or it would end up twenty feet straight down in the hard dirt.

"Are you going to fly or not?" Vern asked.

Maggie held up one hand to admire her green finger-

1

nails and to blow on them, although they were dry. When she got the other hand done, she was going to make herself some rings out of clover. She loved to have beautiful hands because you could admire them so easily.

She showed her hand to Vern. "What do you think?"

"Are you going to fly or not?" Vern asked again.

Junior did not answer. His body was getting ready. He could actually feel strength seeping into his arms. The wings were actually becoming part of him, like a bird's.

This was the third time Junior had climbed up on the barn and allowed Vern to tie on his wings, the third time he had inched his way out to the edge of the roof. But this was the first time he had felt his body actually getting ready to participate, the first time strength had flowed into his arms.

His tongue flicked over his dry lips.

"He's not going," Vern said. His voice was heavy with scorn. "He just wants us to stand out here and beg him."

Maggie said, "Give him time."

"That's what we been doing. Every afternoon we been giving him . . ."

He trailed off because he knew from past experience that it was impossible to predict what Junior would actually do. Junior was going to be a stuntman when he grew up, and sometimes he did things to prove he could, like go down Red Hill on a car made of an apple crate and two skates. "Good-bye, Red Hill," Junior had called, letting go with one hand to wave. Other times, like the day he had pretended he was going over White Run Falls with an inflated garbage bag under each arm—that had come to nothing.

Since there was no way of being sure, Vern waited. In

his boredom he tried to blow a bubble with his gum, but his gum was five days old. Vern was going to chew it for a solid week. Since the second day it had been like chewing a rubber band. The only way he could have any fun with it now was to pull it out and twist it around his tongue. He did this without taking his eyes off Junior.

"Junior, you going or not?" he called.

Junior kept watching the grassy patch between the cornfield and the road.

Maggie finished her other hand, but it wasn't as nice as the first one. She had gone out of the nails in three places. "I couldn't stand to be left-handed, could you?" she asked Vern.

Vern put his gum back into his mouth. He was standing on one leg now, like a flamingo, with the other foot braced on his knee.

Junior took a deep breath, filling his lungs with warm country air—it couldn't hurt to have your lungs inflated with air when you jumped. The thought of his lungs as balloons was comforting to him. Maybe he wouldn't even need the wings. Maybe he would just float. What a surprise that would be. Vern and Maggie—

Vern saw the expression on Junior's face. "He's going." He spoke in the muted voice he used on the rare occasions when he got to the movies and didn't want to disturb the people around him. He'd sit there, gripping the armrests, telling himself what was going to happen: "He's going to crash. . . . He's going to get his head blowed off," until he did disturb somebody and they said, "Will you shut up!"

Maggie looked up from her nails. The top of the Magic Marker was in her mouth, so her mouth looked like a small green circle. She removed it. "Don't hurt yourself, Junior," she called.

Junior nodded without taking his eyes from the grassy clearing. He now thought of the clearing as his destination, the way a pilot thinks of an airport. He could see the very spot—that deep patch of clover—where he would touch down.

Vern knew that just before Junior flew, he would call "Good-bye, Barn." Everyone in the family had tried to break Junior of the habit of saying good-bye to houses and trees and barns, but no one had succeeded.

"It's stupid," Vern had told him. "They can't hear you."

"Maybe, maybe not," Junior had answered, closing his eyes in an expression that made him look, he thought, wise.

Junior exhaled and took another of his deep, inflating breaths. Then he paused. Something beyond the clearing had caught his attention.

A small cloud of dust was moving on the road. Junior watched it first with irritation. Pap was coming home early.

Every Monday afternoon Pap went into town with a truckload of beer and pop cans, which they collected from Highway 123 and gas station trash cans and picnic areas. Today Pap must have sold them fast and was already coming home.

Junior knew he would have to fly right this minute or wait till tomorrow. And he didn't want to do either. He felt he was almost ready—maybe another ten minutes and he would actually fly.

Frown lines came between his eyebrows as he squinted into the distance. He attempted to bring one hand up to

4

shield his eyes so he could see better. He had forgotten this was not possible while you were wearing wings. It was also not possible to wipe the sweat off your chin or scratch where you itched.

He leaned forward slightly.

Seeing the forward motion, mistaking it for a step off the roof, Vern cried, "He's going!"

Junior stopped at the edge of the roof. He saw now that it was not Pap's truck. Pap's truck would be raising more dust. Pap's truck rattled louder than that. Pap's truck didn't have a shiny new bumper. Pap's truck didn't have a blue light on top.

He took one step backward. His wings dragged on the worn roof. He could see what it was now. He gasped with fear. "It's—it's—"

"What's wrong this time?" Vern said. "What's your big excuse this time? Coward! Yellow-belly! Either you jump or I'm going in the house, and I'm not kidding. And I'm not coming back either. I knew you weren't going to fly. You're nothing but a lousy yellow-bellied coward!"

"It's—it's—"

Junior raised one white wing to point to the dusty road. His eyes looked over their heads. He had stopped breathing. He was like a statue pointing. *The Winged Sentinel.*

And then he said one of the most dreaded words in the family vocabulary:

"Police!"

Running Scared

❧ ❧ ❧

"POLICE!" JUNIOR SCREAMED AGAIN.

"Police?" Maggie said.

She got to her feet like a startled deer. She heard in the distance the hum of an unfamiliar engine, an engine perfectly maintained, ready to give chase. "It *is* the police."

"Let's get out of here," Vern said. As he started to run he shouted, "Hide, Junior!"

Maggie flicked her braids over her shoulders and followed. She and Vern ran for their lives, around the barn, past the house, down the gully where Pap threw the household trash. Stumbling over rusty fenders, old bottles, rotten wood, papers, they headed for the woods.

"Wait!"

They barely heard Junior's desperate cry. They ducked through the trees. They knew these woods because they had been running through them all their lives, running from each other mostly, but now it was as if all that had been practice for this moment.

Without a word they dodged through the trees. At the creek they skidded down the bank and jumped together. They kept running.

Not until they were three miles into the woods, past the ravine, did they stop. Then, by mutual unspoken consent —they both knew they were too far into the woods for the police to follow—they flung themselves down on the soft green moss.

Vern had landed on his back and was lying with his eyes shut, mouth open, hands crossed over his chest. He was breathing so hard and fast, his throat stung.

Maggie was wincing, holding her side because everytime she ran fast, it hurt. Her green-tipped fingers pressed hard into the flesh beneath her jeans.

Maggie played different solitary games in different parts of the thick, untouched forest. Here, in this pine-ringed clearing, was where she usually played Hiawatha, but Indian games were not on her mind today.

She was the first one to get her breath. "What do you think?"

Vern couldn't speak yet. He shook his head without opening his eyes.

"What do you think they wanted?" Maggie asked.

Again Vern shook his head.

"Maybe it wasn't the police," Maggie said. "Did you ever think of that?"

"It was the police," Vern managed to say.

"We didn't see them. I didn't. All I heard was Junior yelling 'Police!' Maybe he did that to keep from flying. Maybe it was just—oh, some person who'd turned into our road by mistake."

"Junior wouldn't lie about something like that. It sure sounded like a police car."

High in a tree a woodpecker worked on an old limb.

Maggie kept thinking. She was trying to come up with

some optimistic reason for the arrival of the police. She couldn't. Finally she said, "Maybe Pap was in an accident."

Again Vern shook his head, this time because he didn't think that was what had happened.

"Maybe dead."

Another head shake.

"Then what?" she asked impatiently.

Vern lifted his shoulders and let them fall. Slowly, with great effort, he sat up.

Suddenly he was aware that his chewing gum—his constant companion for five days—was missing. He didn't know if he had swallowed it or if it had popped out while he was running. He opened his eyes.

Maggie's side felt better, so she lay down beside him. She crossed her braids over her chest. Squinting up at the bright July sky, she asked again, "What do you think?"

Vern's mind had started working. This time he shook his head because he was thinking and didn't want to be disturbed.

When he had first heard the cry "Police!" from the top of the barn, he had had only one reaction, an instant reaction—run.

He had not questioned it or thought about it. It was the exact same reaction his grandfather would have had. Running from the police was the only intelligent thing for a Blossom to do. The police might have been put on earth to help some people, but never a Blossom.

"I think that they were looking for Pap to arrest him," Vern said finally.

"Why? What do you think he did? Could it be because his license plate's no good?"

"They don't arrest you for that. They give you tickets."

"Maybe they know that Pap's been making booze in the basement."

"Maybe."

"What are we going to do, Vern?"

Vern scratched his head. When he was six years old, he blew off half of one finger. He had found a dynamite cap, an interesting black cylinder, and, not knowing what it was, had tried to break it open to see what was inside.

He took a sort of pride in his finger, and was glad when some kid asked him what had happened to it. His happiest moment in school had come on the first day of second grade.

The teacher had explained second grade and all the interesting things they would be doing, and then she had said, "Any questions, boys and girls?"

The boy next to Vern raised his hand.

"Yes?" the teacher asked.

"My question is, What happened to that boy's finger?"

"Dynamite," Vern answered.

"What are we going to *do?*" Maggie asked again. She knew that when Vern scratched his head with his dynamited finger, he was thinking hard.

"I'm not through thinking," he said.

Junior's Miss

❧　❧　❧

"WAIT!"

From his desperate perch atop the barn Junior watched them go.

"Wait for me! You guys wait for me!" he cried. "Wait!"

His brother and sister disappeared into the trees, and Junior's heart sank like a stone.

His heart felt so low, he wanted to put his hand on his chest to make sure it had not actually dropped into his stomach, that it was still in his chest where it was supposed to be. He would have done this if it had not been for the wings.

The police car was out of sight now, driving through the stretch of pine trees by the creek. Junior heard the rattle of boards as the car drove slowly over the old board bridge.

Black crows called a warning and flew out of the trees toward the barn. They glided so close, Junior could hear the rush of their wings.

Suddenly, in a panic, Junior swirled and dived for the door to the loft. His wings stopped him at the sill. He fell back with a cry of frustration and fear.

He began tearing at his wings, trying to grab them through the cloth that covered his hands. It was as if the wings were actually part of his body. They wouldn't move.

The strings! He got one in his teeth and pulled so hard, he got the first loose tooth of his life, something he had been waiting for for years. He did not notice.

His brother, Vern, had tied all the knots and spit on them. "Now," Vern had said, "there's no way those are coming loose." Vern knew what he was talking about.

"Get off my arms!" Junior begged the wings. He was beginning to cry now. "Get off!"

He was more desperate than he had been the time the hornets got after him, only he had been able to outrun them. He was fast enough to outrun anything in the whole world, but he couldn't do a thing with these horrible wings on his arms. They were like traps.

And, he went on, tears filling his eyes, he would rather have hornets after him any day in the week than the police.

"Get *off!*"

The police car was coming around the curve now, pulling into the clearing by the barn. Junior could see it, and he dropped to his knees. He crouched against the side of the barn, hiding behind his wings.

The car passed the barn and stopped in front of the house. Junior could hear the doors slam as the police got out of the car.

Tears were running down his cheeks. He was choking silently on his sobs. He was so full of tears, he thought he was going to drown. It was worse than the time he almost did drown down at the creek, trying to stay underwater longer than Vern.

"Anybody home?" one policeman called. He tried to ring the door bell, but it had not worked in ten years. He rattled the screen door.

"Don't let them see me," Junior pleaded. His head was buried beneath his wings. "Please don't let them see me. I'll be good for the rest of my life if you just don't let them see me. I'll give you a hundred million dollars if you don't let them see me."

"I'll check around back," one policeman said.

"I'll check the barn."

Barn! As soon as the word was spoken Junior's wings began to flutter.

"Nobody back here," the policeman called as he rounded the house. His voice was comfortingly far away.

Then, from inside the barn, right below Junior's trembling wings, the policeman called, "Nobody in here either."

Junior could hear the policeman walking around, kicking old straw as if he hoped to find somebody hiding underneath. Junior felt he knew the exact second the policeman looked up at the loft, deciding whether to climb the ladder.

Junior held his breath. Then the policeman walked out and stood exactly where Vern had stood, waiting for Junior's flight.

"Well, what do you think? Think we ought to wait?"

The other policeman joined him, standing in Maggie's place. Across the yard the patrol car's radio sputtered with sound, and Junior pleaded silently, *Somebody's calling you! Go answer!*

12

The policemen stayed where they were, by the barn, one in Maggie's place, one in Vern's.

And, Junior thought with another anxious flutter of his wings, the reason Maggie and Vern had picked that spot was because it was where they had the best view of him on the roof.

"We can come back later."

"Right."

Still they stood there. Why didn't they go? Junior wanted to peer around his wings, but he was not going to do that until they were a million miles away. No, a billion miles away. If he just stayed absolutely still . . .

"What's that up there on the roof?"

Junior's heart stopped beating.

"Where?"

"Up there."

Maybe they meant the house roof, Junior thought, his wings trembling so hard, it was as if they were real. His thoughts bounded frantically in his brain. Please let them mean the house roof. Please—

"Up there."

"On the barn?"

"Yes."

"Is it some kind of kite? What is that thing?"

"That's what I was asking you."

At that moment, the worst moment of his life, Junior felt himself begin to slide. He tried to catch himself. He gave one frantic lurch, but somehow this left him doubled over, his wings pinned beneath him.

He picked up speed. He might as well have been on a sled. He began a long, high-pitched scream. He was sliding facedown, and somehow this made it even scarier.

Another frantic lunge flipped him over, and he looked up into the blinding July sun. He was now on the very spot where he had stood with such hope only moments before.

He was at the edge of the roof, his legs dangling in space. He tottered there, as if on a seesaw, and then he went over.

As he fell his arms rose from his sides, and he began desperately to beat the air with them. He had a brief startlingly clear picture of himself taking flight, soaring over the policemen's heads to the grassy clearing and then beyond, actually skimming the sky like a bird.

Good-bye, World.

The beautiful vision ended as he hit the hard ground at the feet of the startled policemen.

Broken Wings

VERN AND MAGGIE WERE CREEPING UP ON THE HOUSE IN the darkness. They were on their stomachs, edging forward on their elbows like soldiers.

The only sounds were the chirping of the crickets and tree frogs and the occasional whine of a hungry mosquito.

They paused in the shadows. Ahead of them the moonlight turned the clearing white.

"Well, their car's gone," Maggie said.

"Maybe it's parked in a different place."

"There are no lights on in the house," she said, trying to make things better. "Wouldn't they put lights on if they were inside?"

"Not if they were trying to catch us off-guard."

"Oh."

This exchange and Maggie's soft "Oh" gave Vern a feeling of manliness, of being in charge. He felt he alone understood the wiles of policemen, the tricks they played on the innocent. It was going to be up to him to save them all.

He paused to give their secret whistle, to alert Junior

they were in the yard. *Bobwhite! Bobwhite!* The whistle hung on the air like the actual song of a bird.

They waited.

There was no answering call from Junior.

"Stay here," Vern said.

In a crouch he ran through the moonlit clearing and into the bushes around the house. These bushes were as old as the house—seventy years old; and they were so overgrown, a four-door car could disappear in their branches.

Vern ran around to the front of the house behind the bushes. He went up the steps silently, taking them one by one. From the top step he slipped across the porch.

The porch swing had been raised last fall. Pap stored it by pulling it up to the ceiling so it couldn't bang against the house during winter storms. This spring he had not gotten around to letting it down.

Vern paused under the swing, listening.

Then he lifted his head and peered into the room. Everything was still.

He duck-walked to the door and paused at the screen door. Nothing looked out of order. The house smelled the way it always did. At this point he almost felt he could, like his grandfather and his grandfather's dog, Mud, smell a stranger if one was inside.

In a soft voice he said, "Junior?"

There was no answer.

Vern opened the door and went inside.

Like a shadow he moved through the rooms. "Junior," he said softly in each one. Junior might have hidden himself in a closet or under a bed.

It was too dark to see, but Vern knew every stick of

16

furniture in every room. He could have gone through this house blindfolded. In his lifetime not one single piece of furniture had been bought, nothing had been recovered, nothing had been painted, no new curtains had been hung. He felt the comfort of the familiar, almost—it seemed—friendly sofas and beds and chairs.

He opened the basement door. "Junior." There was the familiar smell of warm, fermenting mash, but no Junior.

In the back of the house Maggie waited with her chin resting on her hands. A mosquito, whining, landed on her cheek. She slapped it away.

It was too dark to see her green Magic Marker nails, but if she could have, it would not have brought her one bit of pleasure. She was going to scrub the green off as soon as she could get to the kitchen sink. Green nails were stupid and childish, and she somehow felt she had matured enormously just in the space of that afternoon.

Vern came through the darkness so silently that she gasped out loud when he dropped down beside her.

"I think they're gone."

"But where's Junior?"

"I don't know. He's not in the house."

"Do you think they caught Junior?"

The way she choked on the word *caught* made it sound like the worst thing that could happen to a person.

"Let's check the barn. Maybe he got inside and hid in the straw. That's what he should have done—that's what I meant for him to do when I yelled 'Hide!' " He added with a sigh, "Only, you know Junior."

"Yes."

"And keep quiet."

"All I said was 'Yes.' "

"Well, don't say it so loud. Those policemen could be anywhere."

"Anyway, I don't think he could hide with those wings on his arms," Maggie whispered.

Since this was the exact thing Vern was thinking, he said, "I asked you to be quiet."

In silence they crossed the yard to the barn, running through the moonlit clearing. They slipped behind the old sagging door.

This door hadn't been closed in five years. Even when their mom was home from the rodeo with her horse, Sandy Boy, they didn't close the door. The patch of weeds that grew behind the door was stiff and thorny and reached to their waists.

"Ow," said Maggie.

Vern looked at her in disgust, and she said, "Well, I stuck myself on a thorn." She put her knuckle into her mouth to ease the pain.

Vern peered out around the barn door. "Come on, let's go in."

They slipped around the barn door and stopped short.

"Oh, Vernon," Maggie said, using his full name for the first time in years.

She reached for his hand. He reached for hers, but they were so upset, they did not touch. Their hands grabbed the air.

For in the moonlight, just beneath the spot where Junior had stood poised for flight, lay two broken, twisted, ruined objects, the saddest objects either Maggie or Vern had ever seen.

"Wings," they said together.

18

2,147 Beer and Pop Cans

PAP WAS IN THE CORNER CELL OF THE CITY JAIL. IT WAS one o'clock in the morning, but Pap was not sleeping. He was sitting on his bunk, leaning over his knees, staring at nothing.

His brows were pulled low over his dark eyes. The blood was pumping so hard in his head, the blue veins were throbbing.

Pap was seventy-two years old, and this was the first time he had been arrested. It had been so upsetting that at first he had had to hold himself back from jumping up and actually trying to tear the bars off his cell. If he had been a younger man, at the peak of his strength, that is exactly what he would have done.

Now he sat without moving, except for the veins pumping in his head, and his elbows, which trembled against his legs. He had been sitting like this for five hours.

The arrest had happened so fast, it still bewildered him to think about it.

He had been coming up Sumter Avenue, minding his own business, stopping for stop signs, red lights, and pedestrians. He had to do this because he had an expired license plate, and he did not want to call attention to himself.

He also had 2,147 beer and pop cans in the back of his truck in see-through plastic bags. This was the biggest haul Pap had ever made—the result of a July Fourth weekend bonanza.

It was such a mountain of cans that it caused heads to turn all up and down Sumter Avenue. Pap was proud of it. He got five cents for every can he brought in, and so in the back of his truck was $107.35 cold cash. He had multiplied it out on a brown paper bag. He couldn't wait to get to the station and reap his rewards.

Beside him on the seat was his dog, Mud. Mud was also enjoying the ride. He was looking out the window, doing what Pap called smiling.

Mud had been Pap's dog for ten years, and when Pap was feeling good, Mud felt good. When Pap was low, Mud crawled under the porch and would not come out even if somebody called "Supper!"

Pap turned the corner and started up the steepest part of Spring Street. He was whistling.

Suddenly the car in front of him unexpectedly stopped to back into a parking place. Pap didn't crash into the back of the car, as he felt he certainly had a right to do, but he had to brake so hard that the back of the pickup truck flopped down.

Pap heard a soft, rustling thud as the first bag of beer and pop cans tumbled onto Spring Street. It was a slow-motion kind of thing; the bag just toppled slowly onto the street. Then there was a second thud, and a third.

Pap cussed and pulled up his hand brake, and the old

Chevrolet truck shuddered and died. Pap got out to see the damage.

He stood in the middle of the street, hands braced on the small of his back. He looked at the sorry spectacle of his bags of cans lying on the street. He was wagging his head back and forth.

At that moment two teenaged boys in a Toyota cut around the corner. Pap turned with a frown. The boys ran into the bags like kids hitting a leaf pile. It looked to Pap like they had done it on purpose.

The boys were laughing. The driver threw the Toyota into reverse, U-turned, and took off.

Pap reached into the back of his truck for his shotgun. He fired one shot at the retreating Toyota, but he hit the traffic light down the street. It exploded and left some wires sizzled and popping over the Sumter Avenue intersection.

Two of the bags were busted, and Pap was standing over them, worrying about his $107.35, when he saw some people on the sidewalk. He turned to the people with a frown. He was thinking about asking for some help, even though asking for help was hard for him.

The people, however, thought he was pointing the shotgun at them. They divided. Half of them ran into the nearby Woolco, the other half into Winn Dixie.

The stupid fools! Couldn't they see it was a single-barrel shotgun? All he had wanted was some help, and he didn't even want that now; wouldn't let them help if they asked. Stupid fools!

He was trying to gather up the cans and get them back into the truck by himself when the police arrived—two carloads, sirens screaming.

21

"What's happened?" Pap wondered aloud. He thought maybe there was a bank robbery up the street.

But the police, guns out of their holsters, were advancing on him!

"Wait," he said. He took two steps backward. "I ain't done nothing. I just want to get my cans and get out of here. I just—"

They never let him finish. Two of the policemen grabbed him and shoved him facedown onto the bags of cans. Pap tried to get up.

The policemen were doing something to his arms. Pap didn't want them to. Suddenly Pap felt the bags break, and he heard cans rolling.

"My cans!" Pap cried. He was struggling in the cans now, sending them on their way faster.

The policemen got him to his feet, took his shotgun, handcuffed him, and threw him into the back of a police car. At one time it would have taken the entire police force to do this, but that was before Pap became seventy-two years old.

They started the police car and drove away while the people were coming out of Woolco and Winn Dixie. One by one the people lined up to tell the policeman with the notepad about Pap threatening them.

All this time the 2,147 pop and beer cans were rolling down Spring Street, across the Sumter intersection, and through the municipal parking lot. From there they rolled into White Run Creek. They were clicking like wood chimes.

In White Run Creek they started downstream, bobbing with the currents, turning the creek silver where the sun hit them.

See-Through Eyelids

IT WAS TUESDAY MORNING. JUNIOR WAS DREAMING, AS he always did just before he woke up, that he could see through his eyelids.

This dream had become so real to Junior that he believed he could actually do it. Without opening his eyes, he could see his room and his window and the tree outside the window and the beautiful picture of his mother on Sandy Boy. In the picture his mother was leaning off the back of the horse, upside down, one foot in a strap behind the saddle. Sometimes Junior turned the picture around so he could see his mother right side up.

One time, in first grade, the teacher had said, "Now, boys and girls, I want you all to close your eyes because I want you to imagine something."

Dutifully Junior had closed his eyes and he had, through his eyelids—he was willing to swear this on a stack of bibles—through his eyelids he had seen Mrs. Hodges adjust her brassiere.

This morning he knew, without opening the first eye, that he was somewhere he did not want to be. Beneath him the sheets were stiff and clean. There was a funny smell in the air. There was too much light. Somewhere outside the room a lot of people were doing stuff. Wheels were rolling. Ladies and men talking. A dread fell over him like a cover.

He opened his eyes and gasped with fear. It was the first time in his life he had awakened and not known where he was. He was either in a hospital or a prison, maybe a prison hospital. He had watched enough television to figure that out.

"I got to get out of here," he muttered.

He tried to sling his legs over the side of the bed, but they wouldn't go. It was as if his legs were actually attached to the foot of the bed. He sat up, threw back the sheet.

His legs were in white stiff things. They wouldn't budge. It was yesterday all over again, only now it was his legs that wouldn't work instead of his winged arms.

He began to cry. Under the white stiff things, where he couldn't get at them, his legs hurt. They hurt a lot. Just trying to sling them over the side of the bed had made pain shoot through his whole body.

"What's wrong?"

Junior couldn't have been more startled if God had spoken to him. He had not even been aware that anyone else was in the room. He glanced around so fast, his neck popped.

A redheaded boy in the next bed was watching him with interest.

"I don't know," Junior gasped.

"You must have been in an accident."

25

All the horror came back to him then. "I fell off a barrrr-rrn," he wailed. He flung himself back against his pillow.

"A barn?"

Junior twisted his head from side to side, too miserable now to speak.

"What were you doing on a barn? Making like a rooster? *Er-er-errrrrrrrr-err!*" The boy flapped his arms at his sides.

Junior nodded, dumb with misery and pain.

"You were playing rooster? No kidding? You could go on *That's Incredible.*"

"I wasn't playing rooster. I was trying to fly."

"Did you?"

"Not farrrrr."

"How far? Ten feet? Twenty?"

The distance was so short, Junior could measure it with his hands. He showed the boy a distance of about three feet, then he let his hands drop to his sides.

He wiped his tears on his bed sheet. "Where are we?" he asked the boy.

"Alderson General Hospital, fourth floor."

Junior looked at the boy with grudging admiration. Here was someone who obviously knew a thing or two about hospitals.

"How did I get here?"

"They brought you down from the operating room last night, eleven o'clock. It woke me up. You were moaning. *Oh, no, no, noooooooooo.* Like that. The nurse said you broke both your legs, but she didn't say how."

"The barn."

Pity crept into Junior's voice. He wondered if he would ever again be able to say the word *barn* without wanting to weep.

"Don't you remember anything?"

Junior shook his head.

"They must have knocked you out. Or did they just go ahead and set your legs while you were awake?"

"I don't remember."

"Well, you'd remember if they'd knocked you out. You know how they do it? The doctor takes a great big hammer and he hides it behind his back and then he says, 'Look over there! Quick! What's that?' And when you look, he brings out the hammer and hits you over the head."

"That's not true," Junior said.

"Yes, it is. You know what they did to me?"

"No."

"They cut my head open and filled it with marbles. You can hear them rolling around when I shake my head."

"That's not true."

"Prove it," the boy said.

Junior was too busy going over his own memories to worry about the boy's marbles. To himself he said, *I was up on the barn and the police drove in the yard—I remember that, and I was hiding from them on the roof—I remember that, and I slipped.*

To the boy he added, "If I had been able to go off the roof the way I'd planned, sort of launch myself, I could have escaped over the trees, but they got me all mixed up." Again sorrow made his voice quiver. "It was the police that made me fall."

"You probably wouldn't have flown anyway. People have not had a lot of luck with homemade wings. I saw a whole show that was nothing but people trying to fly— one man had a bicycle with wings on it and he pedaled it

27

right off a cliff. Another man went off a bridge. You were probably lucky just to break two legs."

"That's all I've got." More pity.

"You've got other bones, though—hipbones, jawbones, backbones."

It reminded Junior of a song they sang in first grade: *"Dem bones, dem bones, dem dryyyyy bones."* He never had liked that song.

"You know what they do to you if you break your jawbone, don't you?"

"No."

"Wire your mouth shut so you can't eat for a month."

"That's not—"

A cart rolled by the door. Junior, startled, broke off his sentence to swing his head around. "What was that?"

"When they take you to surgery, they put you on one of those carts."

"I'm not getting on a cart," Junior said instantly. "No matter what happens, no matter what they say, I'm not getting on any cart."

"If you won't get on the cart, then they bring the hammer in the room and hit you over the head right here. They did it to that boy that was in that bed right over there. I saw them. They had to hit him twice. One time he put his hand up to protect his head, and they hit him on the hand. He took his hand down, and they hit him on the head so hard, his eyes popped out."

"That's not t—"

Again Junior didn't get to finish what he was saying, because the nurse came in. He seemed to get smaller as he realized she was coming to his bed.

"Good morning."

28

The nurse handed Junior a tiny paper cup. He muttered "Thank you" before he saw there was a pink pill in it. Junior looked at it with suspicion.

"What's that?"

"It's your medicine," the nurse said.

Junior let the pill roll around in the cup. Sometimes Maggie played nurse with him, but she used catsup for medicine.

"Now, open wide," Maggie would say. She'd pour some catsup into a tablespoon, hold his nose, and poke the catsup in.

He loved to play patient, but he didn't want to be one. Suddenly he was homesick. Maggie made a better nurse than anybody in this whole hospital. Tears filled his eyes.

The boy in the next bed said, "If you don't take your pill, they bring in a great big needle—thaaat long, and they give you a shot in your rear end."

"Now, Ralphie," the nurse warned, "you shouldn't scare Junior. He hasn't even been here one—"

Before she could finish, Junior had swallowed his pink pill. "Water?" He shook his head.

He handed the nurse the empty cup, lay back, and closed his eyes. For the first time in his life he was glad not to have see-through eyelids.

Going to Town

❦   ❦   ❦

"I'M TIRED," MAGGIE SAID.

Vern said, "Keep walking."

"I can't. My flip-flop's broken."

"Fix it."

"Well, stop and give me a chance."

Without turning around, Vern stopped. He put his hands in his pockets. He sighed with impatience. He stared ahead at the road. Beyond the curve and the pointed pine trees a huge red sun was sinking. Vern was not admiring the view. He sighed again, louder. "We have a long way to go. We haven't even crossed the Interstate yet."

Maggie sat on the side of the road and pushed the worn piece of plastic back into the sole of her flip-flop. Then she slipped her dirty foot through the thong. Without getting up, she said, "I think we ought to call Mom."

"No."

"Why not?"

"I told you. We are only supposed to call if it's an emergency. You know that. The last thing Mom said was for us not to be calling all the time."

"This *is* an emergency."

"An emergency is what we can't handle ourselves."

"That's what this is. We can't handle this. Pap may be in jail."

"We can handle it."

Vern did not turn around during this conversation. He just faced the sunset. His mouth was a straight line in his tired face.

The reason Vern spoke with such firmness about not calling their mom was that the week before, he had tried to call her himself. He had wanted to hear her voice so much that he had walked three miles to the Exxon station and stepped into the pay phone booth.

Every week their mom wrote postcards to let them know where she would be staying. Their mom still went on the rodeo circuit in the summers—she was a trick rider; and she never knew exactly what motel she would be staying at till she got there.

In Vern's hand was the latest postcard, the latest phone number.

When their dad was alive, they all went on the circuit. They had had a camper, and all three kids had slept on a table that made into a bed. Their parents slept over the cab.

Vern, who was old enough to remember those days, thought they were the happiest days of his life. Just one long stretch of dusty, interesting days and bright nights. Even the rainy days and the mud had been fun.

Vern had looked again at the number. His mom was staying this week at the Paisano Motel. There was a picture of a long brick motel with a sign shaped like a som-

31

brero. The number was printed in big letters. He dialed them.

"Is this a credit card call?" the operator asked.

"No, I've got money," he said. The money was lined up on the shelf under the phone—quarters, then dimes, then nickels, neat as a bank.

"Deposit three dollars and thirty cents."

It took Vern a long time to get that much money into the phone, but it was worth it. Immediately the phone began to ring and a voice said, "Paisano Motel."

Vern cleared his throat. "Could I speak with Vicki Blossom?"

"Who?"

"Vicki Blossom. She's staying there."

"She's not registered."

"She has to be."

"Nope. No Blossom."

"She's with the rodeo."

"Honey, everybody staying at this motel is with the rodeo."

"But this is my mom. She gave me this number."

He was horrified to hear his voice break on the word *mom.* Now the motel manager would think he was a child. If his mom did come, she would say, "Your little boy called. He sounded like he was crying."

In a mature, adult voice he said, "Well, if she does check in, would you tell her Vern called, and everything is all right here."

"I will, hon."

"Thank you."

"You're welcome."

He stood, hands in his pockets, staring down the highway. The shadows were getting longer. The traffic was getting sparse. Everybody was either home for supper or going home for supper but them.

Maggie got to her feet. "I still think we ought to call."

Vern swirled around. Remembering the incomplete phone call made his eyes even harder. "I told you I can handle it!"

"Well, I'm the oldest and I ought to be the one to decide when we handle it and when we don't."

"Look, you want to call—go ahead. Be my guest. Call."

At that moment he looked so much older than Maggie that the eleven months that separated them might as well have been eleven years. He stared at her with eyes that did not blink once.

Maggie blinked seven or eight times. She said, "Vern, I can't call. I don't have any monnnnnney."

He turned and started walking. To Maggie it was the way John Wayne walked into the sunset when he wasn't coming back. Quickly she got to her feet.

"Wait for meeeeeee."

Vern kept walking.

Maggie hopped on one foot to get her flip-flop adjusted. Then she ran down the warm asphalt road after him.

Mud

❦ ❦ ❦

EVERY TIME PAP SLAMMED ON THE BRAKES OF THE Chevrolet, four things happened. The tailgate dropped, the sun visors flopped down, the glove compartment opened, and Mud slid onto the floor.

This time Mud was so surprised at the sudden stop that he struck the tender part of his throat on the door of the glove compartment. Then with a yelp of pain he slid to the worn floor.

His throat felt as if something were caught inside, and he gagged-coughed a few times. He looked with interest at the small wad of spit he had coughed up on the floor. Then he jumped on the seat to look around.

Pap was outside the truck. Mud jumped nimbly out the door and joined him. Pap paid no attention to Mud, but Mud was used to that. Pap knew he was there.

The next few moments were beyond Mud's ability to understand. There was a crash, a shot, and then a struggle that sent beer cans rolling down the street and Mud under the Chevrolet.

When he realized some men were struggling with Pap,

hurting him, he darted out to help. A kick from one of the policemen sent him back under the truck. Stray cans shot at him, scared him, sent him further back.

He waited between the front wheels of the truck. He was panting with alarm, his ears flat on his broad head, his golden eyes wild.

After a moment he crawled on his belly to the driver's side of the truck. He thought it might be a good idea to get inside. The door had been closed.

Still keeping close to the pavement, he went to the back of the truck. He looked out. He didn't see Pap anywhere.

He was getting ready to jump into the truck and lie down on a gunnysack when the tow truck arrived. As soon as the huge hook clanged under the truck's bumper, Mud started running.

He ran right down the middle of Sumter Avenue, on the yellow line, his ears flying behind him, his tail low. "That stupid dog's going to get hit!"

"Maybe he's rabid!"

"Someone ought to call the dogcatcher."

Mud kept running for five blocks until he came to an intersection, and then he turned left on a red light, causing curses and the squealing of brakes.

Mud was usually cautious about traffic because he had been hit by a car when he was six weeks old. That's how he had become Pap's dog in the first place. He and his mother—a big yellow farmer's dog named Minnie—had been chasing cars along County Road 26. His mother was a great car chaser, and the first thing all her pups learned was to chase cars.

Mud had inherited from his mother a lot of natural ability for chasing cars, but he still had a lot to learn.

35

On that particular morning Mud and Minnie had spent a lot of time lying in the shade, waiting for the hum of a motor.

About noon Minnie heard a loud roar. It was a car Minnie particularly liked to chase, a BMW. She got up from her hole under the tree and jumped the ditch. Mud did too.

Minnie got down low in the weeds—she liked to take cars by surprise.

Mud was beside her, down low too. His mother's body was trembling with excitement. His was too.

The car roared into view. Minnie and Mud sprang out of their hiding place.

But this time the car didn't gain speed as it usually did. This time it didn't race Minnie. This time it swerved right at her.

Minnie got out of the way with a graceful, twisting backward dive, but Mud didn't. Mud was hit and flung into a drainage ditch beside the road.

Pap came by about a half hour later, on foot. He was whistling "Camptown Races." He stopped after the first *doo-dah* because he saw Minnie. She was whining and taking anxious steps back and forth at the far side of the ditch.

It was clear to Pap she was worried about something in the ditch.

"Well, let's see what we got here," said Pap.

Mud was so covered with mud that Pap didn't see him at first. Then he said, "Well, well."

He put one foot down in the ditch, and he touched Mud's throat in a certain place to see if he was still alive. When he saw that he was, he said, "Let me help you, pal,"

36

in the same voice he would use if he was helping one of the children.

"Not another dog," the kids' mom had said when she saw him carrying Mud through the doorway.

Pap nodded.

"I wish one time you'd bring home something worth looking at, like a French poodle."

"Where'd you find him, Pap?" Vern asked.

"In the mud. His leg's broke."

"Well, as soon as it heals, you get rid of him. I mean it."

"I know you do."

Mud spent most of the afternoon running around town, dodging cars and trucks and people. At dusk he dropped like a bag of bones under the carryout window of a Dairy Queen. He lay there, so spent, so miserable, that during the evening people began dropping pieces of their hamburgers around him, the way people drop coins into a beggar's hat.

Here was the word he heard again and again, but even if someone had presented him with a sirloin steak, he would not have had the heart to eat it.

Busting Open

✺ ✺ ✺

"WHAT'S WRONG WITH YOU—REALLY?" JUNIOR ASKED.
"I'm serious. I have to know." For two hours Junior had
been trying to get Ralphie to tell him why he was in the
hospital. "I told you what was wrong with me," Junior
went on in a bargaining voice.

"No, you didn't. The nurse did."

Junior said, "Well, I would have."

"You'll find out when I go to therapy."

"What's therapy?"

"Don't you know anything?"

"I guess not." Junior sounded so low that Ralphie re-
lented.

He said, "Oh, all right. Here is what's really and truly
wrong with me. I swallowed watermelon seeds and now
watermelons are growing inside me, and when they get
big, I'm going to bust open."

"No," Junior said.

"When I bust open, you better get out of the way or
you'll get watermelon and guts all over you."

"No!"

"After I bust open, they're going to put a zipper in my stomach so I can zip myself open and shut."

"*No!*"

"Now, Ralphie." It was the nurse again—more little paper cups, more pills. "What lies are you telling Junior this time?"

"He told me he had watermelons inside him and marbles in his head. He told me he was going to bust open and then you were going to put a zipper in him."

Junior tossed his pink pill down like a pro.

"Just don't listen to him, Junior. Don't believe a word he says. He's—"

"Excuse me."

Junior looked up in alarm. Everything about the hospital alarmed him, put him on his guard—carts, needles, hammers; and now a policeman was standing in the doorway. The only good thing so far about being in the hospital had been getting away from the police!

The policeman said exactly what Junior was afraid he would say: "Can I talk to the Blossom boy for a few minutes?"

"Me?" Junior asked. He pulled his covers up higher on his chest. He wanted to pull them over his head.

The policeman nodded and came into the room. "How are you feeling this morning, son?"

"I'm fine." Junior's voice was high and thin as a reed.

"Were you one of the policemen who was there when he fell?" Ralphie asked. He was turned on his side now, propped on his elbow, watching with interest. He did not wear hospital gowns, and he had on a T-shirt that said Genius Inside.

The policeman said, "Yes."

40

"Then why didn't you catch him?"

"What?"

"When he fell, why didn't you catch him?" Ralphie spoke each word as carefully as if he were talking to someone who was dull-witted.

"It all happened pretty fast, son," the policeman said.

"Yeah, but you guys are supposed to be pretty fast, have quick reactions. What if it had been a burglary? If you can't move any quicker than that, you wouldn't even have your gun out till the robbers had escaped. Part of your training should be in fast reactions, *bang-bang;* and if you haven't got them, you should get a desk job or work in a cafeteria. On TV the cops—"

"We do our best, son." The policeman turned his back on Ralphie. "Are your legs giving you a lot of trouble?"

"No," Junior lied.

"They're broken," Ralphie told the policeman's back. "Sure, they're giving him trouble. You think it's fun to have broken legs?"

Junior kept his eyes on the mound his toes made under the sheet. He was very, very grateful to have Ralphie in the next bed. Ralphie was better than a lawyer, taking his side, bringing up points Junior had not even thought of. He would have given Ralphie a look of gratitude, but the policeman was standing between them.

"The reason I was out at your place yesterday afternoon," the policeman was saying, "was because earlier in the day we had to arrest your grandfather."

"Pap?" Now he looked at the policeman.

"Your grandfather was disturbing the peace. He pulled out a shotgun and fired it on Spring Street."

"Did he kill anybody?"

"No."

"Hit anybody?"

"No, but he's in jail, and he's going to have to have a hearing. The hearing's day after tomorrow, and after that, depending on how things go, he's liable to spend a month or two in the county jail."

"Pap? Jail?" Junior couldn't fit the two pictures together. *"Pap? Jail?"*

"He has a right to a court-appointed lawyer," Ralphie said. "By the way, did you read him his rights?"

The policeman ignored Ralphie and gave Junior a look of regret. He took out pencil and paper.

"Now, son, what we need to know is where your mom is and how to get in touch with her. Your grandfather—Pap, as you call him—told me there were two other kids, your brother and your sister"—he checked a notepad—"Maggie and Vern, and we need to know where they are."

Junior looked up at the policeman with his mouth hanging open. He couldn't have said a word if he'd wanted to. It was as if words hadn't even been thought of yet.

Ralphie leaned around the policeman. "Under the law," he said, "you aren't required to tell him—one—single—thing."

"Thank you," said Junior.

The Jailbird

MAGGIE WAS AT THE BUS STOP, SITTING ON THE BENCH
that had been put there by the Parkinson Funeral Home.
She was swinging her legs back and forth.

She wished, as she usually did, that she had on a pair of
cowboy boots. Her mom had bought her lots of boots
when she was little—Maggie even had a picture of herself
coming home from the hospital with a pair of tiny cowboy
boots sticking out from under the blanket.

But this year her mom had said, "Maggie, your feet are
growing so fast, it would just be wasting money."

"I can't go around without boots," Maggie had said. It
was like going around undressed.

"They'd be too little in six months."

"Then buy me a big pair. I'll grow into them. Buy me a
cheap pair at Shoe Mart."

"I don't even have the money for that, shug." Her
mom's voice when she said the word *shug* always sounded
so sad, so regretful, that Maggie could never keep on
begging.

Maggie imagined how much better she would look if

she had boots on now instead of worn green flip-flops. Cowboy boots made any outfit look classy, even a worn T-shirt and cut-off jeans.

Across the street her brother Vern was walking slowly up and down in front of the city jail, pausing every now and then to give the secret birdcall. *Bobwhite. Bobwhite.* Four more steps. *Bobwhite.*

Vern was listening for an answering whistle from inside the jail. This was the only way he could think of to find out if Pap was inside.

He whistled again and waited. His head was cocked to one side, like a bird's, listening.

Maggie thought Vern looked so suspicious, he would probably end up getting arrested himself. No one in his right mind stood in front of the city jail whistling like a bobwhite.

She had said, "Well, it sounds stupid to me." And then because she couldn't think of anything better, she had added, "But go ahead and try it if you don't mind making a fool of yourself."

A bus came by, and the bus driver opened the door for her. "I'm not going anywhere," she called. As the door closed she added, "I wish I was."

The bus passed, and Maggie could see Vern again, at the last window now. She wished that she would look down in the gutter and spot a five-dollar bill. Then she'd go straight to a pay phone.

"Mom," she would say. "We have an emergency."
Bobwhite! Bobwhite!

Maggie was going to be a trick rider like her mom when she grew up. Her dad had been in the rodeo too. He had been World's Champion Single Steer Roper in 1973. He had won $6,259 that year, and they had thought they were on easy street.

The next year he had been killed by a steer in Ogallala, Nebraska, in a rodeo that Maggie could never remember. "Don't you remember us waiting for Mom to get back from the hospital?" Vern sometimes asked in amazement. "We hid under the bleachers."

"No."

"Don't you remember driving home with Mom crying so bad, she drove off the road every few miles?"

"No."

The truth was, Maggie didn't really want to remember. She scratched a mosquito bite on the back of her leg. Then she sat forward, watching her brother with new interest.

Vern was listening to something. He was standing there with one ear turned up to the last high window on the side of the jail.

"Do you hear something?" Maggie called.

She waited until two cars passed, and she ran across the street to join him.

"Do you hear something or are you just acting like you do?"

Vern held up one hand to quiet her.

"I have a right to know if you heard something," she began, but then she stopped. She turned her head, ear up, to the window too.

From inside the jail came the answering call of a bob-white.

"He's in there!" Maggie said. She was as delighted as if she'd discovered he was in the movies. She grabbed Vern's arms and tried to swing him around. He was unyielding.

45

Bobwhite!

"He's in there, all right," Vern said.

"Well, let's go."

"Where?"

"To see him."

"Are you stupid or what? We can't go walking in the police station?"

Bobwhite! Bobwhite! The bobwhite was getting excited now.

"Why not?"

"Because that's exactly what they expect us to do. That's why they didn't bother setting a trap for us at the farm. They knew we'd have to come down here. We walk in and—bam—they get us too."

Bobwhite! Bobwhite!

"Why would they want us, though? That's what I don't understand."

"All I know is that they do. They wouldn't have come to the farm, would they, if they hadn't wanted us? They wouldn't have taken Junior away, would they, if they didn't want him? What we got to find out is why."

"How are we going to do that?"

He held up his dynamited finger. "One. We got to find out what Pap's in jail for." He held up another finger. "Two. We got to find out where Junior is. Three. We got to get them both out."

"How, Vern, how?"

"I'm thinking." And as Vern scratched his head with his dynamited finger, inside the jail the bobwhite kept whistling and whistling and whistling.

With her flip-flop Maggie rubbed the mosquito bite on

46

the back of her leg. "You better answer Pap. He's going to whistle his head off if you don't. . . ."

Maggie trailed off as she looked up at Vern. He was watching her with such intensity that she swallowed. "What is it?" she asked. "What's wrong?"

"I just figured it out."

"What? What are you talking about?"

"We," he said, "are going to have to break into city jail."

Pap's Place

PAP WAS STANDING ON HIS BUNK. HIS FACE WAS TURNED to the patch of light overhead, his window. With shaking fingers he was trying to reach the chain that opened the vent.

"What you trying to do, pops?" someone in the next cell asked. "Don't open the vent 'cause hot air'll come in. The good thing about this jail is the AC."

"The only good thing," someone said down the way.

Pap's fingers trembled an inch below the chain. He stretched higher. Now he was a half inch away. His fingers made scissors movements under the chain.

Bobwhite! The call came again from the sidewalk below. Pap stopped stretching his old bones long enough to put his hand on his chest and answer.

Bobwhite!

"He think he a bird. Man, he think he gone fly out the window," another man said.

"Byyyyye-bye, blackbird," someone sang.

There was amused laughter. Everyone but Pap was a regular and knew one another. Two of them had been

48

arrested together on a drunk and disorderly charge and were playing cards. Another was playing his Japanese transistor radio. Pap was not even aware they were in the same jail with him.

"Gin!" a cardplayer cried.

Up until the moment Pap had heard the call of the bobwhite, he had been in the deepest, blackest despair of his life. If he could have stopped himself from breathing, he would have. He would just have let all the air out of his lungs and not taken any more in. It would have been a relief to everybody and everything—to his worn-out lungs, the police, his disgraced family. *Good riddance* was the expression.

Then came the whistle. He had taught the kids that himself. "Here's what my brothers and me used to do when we wanted to call to each other, like one would be in school and we'd want him to sneak out and go fishing with us and we'd do this: *Bobwhite! Bobwhite!*"

Vern had caught on right away and was now as good as Pap. Maggie was passable, and Junior was, as Pap put it, "getting there."

Hearing that whistle today had made tears come to his eyes, and he hadn't cried in the four years since his son Cotton had died in Ogallala, Nebraska.

Hearing that whistle had been like hearing something from his past and something from his future at the same time. It was the first glimmer of hope Pap had felt since the jail door clanked shut behind him.

In his excitement Pap had not bothered to wipe his tears away, and they were now making small paths down his dusty cheeks, falling easily into the wrinkles like raindrops into a gulley.

Pap's fingers reached again for the elusive chain. He actually touched the metal this time.

"What's he gone do when he gets up there? Ain't nobody skinny enough to get through that little bitty window."

Someone said, "Let him try. Maybe he like Rubber Man, in the funny papers."

Laughter.

"I wish I was the Invisible Man. You wouldn't see me around this place no more."

More laughter.

Pap looked around, not at the man who had spoken but at the man in the next cell who had his radio tuned to Rock 101. With all that racket it was a miracle he had heard the kid's whistle at all. And worse, the loud music might have prevented the kids from hearing his answering whistle.

"Turn that off," Pap said.

"I like it onnnnn." The man with the radio did not bother to open his eyes.

Pap looked up at the window again, then back to the man, then back to the window, bewildered about what to do next.

He heard nothing. Maybe they'd given up. Maybe at this moment they were walking home.

The rock song ended, and in the relative quiet of a commercial Pap heard a bobwhite whistle. It sounded fainter, as if the kids were moving away.

In a desperate move Pap yanked up his mattress. He rolled it into a wad and stood on it. His high-top shoes dug into the filling.

Now he could reach the chain. He pulled it open. Warm

50

air rushed into his face, along with the sounds of a bob-white. Pap threw back his head and gave the answering whistle ten times without stopping.

"He crazy," one of the cardplayers said.

And no one in city jail bothered to argue with the card-player.

Ralphie Goes to Therapy

JUNIOR WAS SLEEPY, BUT EVERY TIME HIS EYES CLOSED he snapped them open. He had to stay awake. He didn't want to miss it when Ralphie went to therapy. Finding out what was wrong with Ralphie was the only thing he had to look forward to.

And yet, like everything in this whole hospital, in this whole world, it would probably be a disappointment. Like lunch. The memory brought tears to Junior's eyes.

All morning long Junior had been looking forward to lunch. When the nurse put his tray down and rolled up his bed and he saw a huge hamburger, he could have jumped up and down with joy—if, of course, it had not been for the broken legs.

He had just picked up the hamburger, which he intended to devour in exactly four bites. A boy in his school was famous for eating a whole hamburger in one bite—Junior had seen him do it. Then the boy would drink his whole milk in one pull on the straw, put his cookies—however many—in his mouth, and go out to recess.

Junior wasn't that good yet. Four bites was his record.

He was just getting ready for the first bite when Ralphie said, "You aren't going to eat that stuff without testing it first, are you?"

Junior stopped with the hamburger at his lips. The smell of the bun had made his mouth water. "Why would I test it?"

"Stupid, to make sure they haven't put medicine in it."

"Medicine." Junior looked down at his hamburger. He closed his mouth.

"Yeah, drugs, you know, to keep you groggy, so they can do things to you."

"Do they really do that?"

"You better believe it."

Junior wasn't as hungry as he thought he was. "Maybe I'll just drink my milk."

"Is it chocolate?"

"Yes."

"Then be double careful."

"Why?" Junior put his milk carton back on his tray, exactly in the little wet square where it had been.

"That's usually their first target. They figure, see, that the kid's going to go for chocolate milk. He probably doesn't get that at home. 'Wow, chocolate milk!' And down the hatch without half tasting it. Either that or the ice cream. Why do you think you get ice cream every single meal?"

Junior didn't know they did. He folded his hands over his chest.

He looked at the items on his tray. It was a nice tray, better than at the school cafeteria. Getting a tray this nice had given him a special feeling.

At school Junior had always had to bring his lunch in a

53

paper bag, and he envied the kids that went through the line and got trays. Now he had thought he was part of that happy privileged group at last.

"What do these drugs taste like?" he asked.

He glanced over at Ralphie. He saw Ralphie was eating his hamburger.

"If it's poison—" Junior began.

"I didn't say poison," Ralphie corrected through a mouthful of hamburger. "I said drugs."

To Junior it was the same thing. "If it's got drugs in it, then why are you eating it?"

"I'm an addict. I need it. It's my fix."

After a long moment Junior picked up one potato chip. He figured it would be hard to get drugs into a potato chip. He progressed slowly, though, nibbling the edges. Maybe it did taste funny.

The nurse came in. She said, "I thought you were so hungry, Junior."

"Not really."

He wondered if he should swallow the funny-tasting potato chip or spit it out.

Ralphie said, "He's scared there's drugs in the food."

"I wonder who could have put that idea in his head," the nurse said. "Junior, your food is not drugged."

"Of course *she'd* say that," Ralphie said.

"Would you like me to take a bite of your hamburger?" Junior nodded.

She broke off a piece and ate it. "Anything else?"

"The milk."

"Well, let me get a straw. Honestly, Ralphie, we're going to have to put you in isolation. You get meaner by the day." She took a sip of milk. "Now do you think you can eat something?"

Junior nodded.

"I'll be back for your trays later."

As she went from the room, Ralphie said, "Sure, she tasted the hamburger and the milk, but she didn't taste the ice cream. You better hand that over to me."

"No way!"

Now, as he lay waiting for Ralphie to go to therapy, he wondered if he had made a serious mistake in eating the ice cream. It had not tasted the way he remembered ice cream tasting.

And he did feel drugged. His eyelids were so heavy, he could not keep them from dropping over his eyes. And he couldn't think straight.

"What time do you go?" he asked drowsily.

"Where?"

"Therapy."

"I've already been, stupid! I'm back."

Junior didn't know whether it was true or not. He couldn't open his eyes to find out.

Junior slept.

Jailbreak

"Break into jail!" Maggie yelled.

"Shut up! You want the police to hear you?"

Maggie lowered her voice. "Break *into* jail? Are you out of your mind? We cannot break *into* jail."

"Yes, we can. Look, it's not like breaking into a bank. The police expect people to break into banks. They have alarms set for people breaking into banks."

"They have alarms in jail too."

"They have alarms for breaking *out* of jail. There's a big difference. Nobody is expecting anybody to break *into* jail. That would be stupid."

"Exactly!"

"Maggie, listen—we have to. There's no other way we can talk to Pap."

"Why don't we call him on the phone?"

"Now you're the one who's out of her mind. You think they let prisoners take phone calls?"

"They let them have one. I saw it on TV."

"Make one. They let them make one—to their lawyer. There's a big difference."

"No way," Maggie said. "I am not breaking into jail."

"All right, you don't have to go. If you're scared, you can wait here. That might be better. Then if I get caught, you'll still be free to help us."

"Vern, couldn't we write him a letter?"

"A letter! Don't you think they open every single letter that comes in the jail? What's your next idea, Maggie— that we bake him a cake with a file in it?"

Tears stung Maggie's eyes. She was tired. She wanted to be home in her bed instead of in front of the city jail.

"I want Mom."

"You think I don't?"

Vern's thin shoulders sagged. He sighed. He jammed his hands deep in his pockets. He said, "All right, you might as well know the worst."

"The worst?" Maggie swung her head around so fast, her braids whipped around her neck. "What worst could there be?"

"Here it is. I tried to call Mom three days ago and she wasn't where she was supposed to be. The Paisano Motel had never heard of her. There's no way in the world we can reach Mom now. Mom's gone."

As soon as Vern said "Mom's gone" Maggie began to sob. She didn't bother covering her eyes. She just threw back her head and bawled.

"Shut up, Maggie. Come on, shut up!" He decided yelling at her wasn't going to work. He lowered his voice. "Please, Maggie, listen. Be quiet. They'll hear you inside the station."

He drew her down the sidewalk away from the door. She followed, her eyes blind with tears. They stopped beneath an elm tree.

"Maggie, please don't cry. Please. You'll make yourself sick. You won't have to go in the jail if you don't want to, and if I don't think it's going to work, if I'm not absolutely sure, I won't go in either."

Maggie kept crying. It was such a relief to be getting some sympathy that she couldn't have stopped if she had wanted to.

"Maggie," he said finally in one last desperate attempt, "I'll buy you some cowboy boots if you stop."

She blinked. "You don't have any money."

"I do."

"With you?"

"Yes."

"How much?"

"Twenty-two dollars and seventy-seven cents."

He remembered suddenly that he had spent three dollars and thirty cents on the incompleted phone call to their mother, but there was no need to mention that. "Pap gave it to me for helping collect pop cans."

"Is that enough for boots?"

"Cheap boots."

Maggie hesitated.

"But the cheap boots look nice, Maggie; even cowboys can't tell them from the expensive ones."

Maggie wiped her tears on her arm.

"Tell me what we're going to do," she said.

More Mud

❧　❧　❧

THE DAIRY QUEEN WAS CLOSED. THE LIGHTS WERE out. The parking lot was empty.

Still Mud lay where he had fallen, beneath the carryout window. He was like a character in a fairy tale who had been put under a wicked, hurtful spell. Around him were the dried offerings of strangers.

The only movement was an occasional twitching of his long, dusty legs. Mud was running in his dreams.

It was the silence that brought Mud to his senses. As long as people had been fussing over him, begging him to eat—"Come on, boy, it's hamburger. See, hamburger!"— it had been easy to lie there, out of it, too unhappy to move. Even when a boy had lifted Mud's lip and poked a piece of bacon cheeseburger inside, Mud had not reacted.

"Don't do that!" the boy's mother had cried, swatting at the boy and hitting Mud.

Mud did not flinch.

Another swat. This time the mother hit her mark, the back of the boy's pants. "Didn't I tell you not to fool with strange dogs? You want to get rabies?"

"Noooooooooooooo . . ."

Now the parking lot was so quiet, Mud could have been the only living creature left in the world. He was awake, and he knew he was going to have to open his eyes.

He opened one. He rolled it up to the Dairy Queen, down to the streetlight.

Then he lifted his head and looked around. He saw nothing that looked familiar. He could not even remember lying down here.

He was not hungry, but it was easier to swallow the scrap of bacon cheeseburger that was already in his mouth than to spit it out. The scrap hit his empty stomach, causing real hunger.

Still he was selective. He ignored all bread that smelled of mayonnaise and all french fries. He separated pickles, onions, tomato, and lettuce from meat and made a discard pile before eating the meat. He ended the meal with a little chocolate shake which someone had thoughtfully poured in the lid of the cup. He licked the excess from his whiskers.

Mud shook himself, stretched, and lifted his leg in the direction of the Dairy Queen. Then he went to the curb and looked both ways. The street was deserted. He ambled to the corner.

There Mud hesitated. He stood with his nose high, smelling the evening air. He took a few steps to the right, then to the left, figuring out which smells came from which direction.

Mud reached a decision. He lifted his leg on the telephone pole, and then, with a sort of ambling gait, he set off in the direction of town.

Mud was a one-man dog. He could not even remember

60

his pre-Pap days when he and Minnie had chased cars, when the farm girls down the road had dressed him and his brother up in doll clothes and played baby with them.

"How's your baby today?"

"It's sick."

"Mine's sick too."

And he and his brother ate medicine made of grass until they could escape and run through the yard, tripping on their dresses.

Mud's life began when Pap reached down in the ditch and took his shivering body in his gentle hands.

In all the years since Mud had recovered from the accident, Pap had taken him everywhere he went. If Pap went to the barn, Mud went to the barn. If Pap got in the truck, Mud got in. On the rare occasions when Pap said "Stay," Mud waited in the back of the truck, curled up on a gunnysack, with his ears turning radarlike for the sound of Pap's shuffling feet.

His job in life, as nearly as he could figure it out, was keeping Pap company.

Now his job was even clearer. He had to find Pap.

He crossed the deserted street, pausing on the yellow line to sniff the evening air.

•

Visitors

ALL THE THINGS JUNIOR WANTED TO INVENT HAD AL-
ready been invented. It was the story of his life. He would
say, "I'm going to invent shoes with little wheels on the
bottom," and before he could describe how people would
roll around like magic on the wheeled shoes, Vern would
sneer, "And what are you going to call them—roller
skates?" Then Junior would remember where he had gotten the idea.

He had, at various times, wanted to invent motorbikes,
pogo sticks, and the harmonica.

"I'm going to invent a tiny little musical instrument,
like a sideways horn, that you blow in, and you can slide it
up and down and get different notes."

"Why don't you call it a harmonica?" Another of Vern's
sneers.

That night, after supper, Junior remembered with tears
in his eyes that he had once almost invented the harmonica. What made him remember was that Ralphie's two
little brothers came to see him and one of them brought
Ralphie a tiny harmonica exactly one inch long. He had
bought the harmonica in a joke store.

As soon as Ralphie began to wheeze out a tune on the harmonica, tears came to Junior's eyes. It wasn't only that some inventor had gotten the idea first and beat him to it. It was that no one had brought him a tiny harmonica. Nobody had brought him anything.

And he didn't have any visitors. He was never going to have any. Maggie and Vern didn't even know where he was. And if they did come, they wouldn't think to bring him a tiny harmonica.

As he lay there, wiping his tears on his top sheet, listening to an off-key chorus of "Dixie" from the next bed, he suddenly wished he had told the policeman where to find Vern and Maggie.

He wished he had said to the policeman, "Look behind the house in the woods. They have a hideout by the ravine." No, he wished he had told the policeman to go in the woods and give the whistle of a bobwhite, and when Vern and Maggie ran out, thinking it was him, the police could grab them.

He wished he had thought to say, "You better bring them here for identification." He wanted to give them a hard, unforgiving look before they were led away to prison.

"What's wrong with you?" one of Ralphie's brothers asked. The brother had been lying in the empty bed across from Junior, pretending he had appendicitis. Now he was sitting up, cross-legged.

While Junior was deciding whether he could tell his story without starting to sob, Ralphie switched his harmonica into his cheek and chanted, "He fell off a roof. He was trying to fly. He hit the ground. He thought he would die. A poem, by Ralph Waldo Smith." Then he blew one loud, piercing chord that used every hole on the harmonica.

After that, having had the whole thing turned into a poem, followed by what sounded like a musical raspberry, Junior didn't feel like saying anything.

"You know what? Now nobody in your family will ever be allowed up on the roof again," the brother said. "Ralphie fell off the riding lawn mower five years ago and cut off his leg and none of us have been allowed on the riding mower since. We can't even sit on it when it's in the garage. Just because *he* was stupid enough to fall off, *we* have to be punished the rest of our lives."

Junior wiped his tears on his sheet, this time because he wanted to get a closer look at Ralphie's brother. "Is that what happened to him?" He nodded his head in the direction of Ralphie's bed.

"Yes. What did he tell you—that a crocodile bit off his leg at Disneyland?"

"He didn't tell me anything."

"That's what he usually tells people, but he's never even been to Disneyland. He fell off a mower, and the mower cut off his leg."

"And," the other brother said, moving into the conversation, "he's had five operations because his bone keeps poking through. He just had one, and now he's getting a new leg. Every time he grows, he has to get a new leg. There's his old one over in the corner. You want to see it?"

Junior nodded.

The brothers had a short tug-of-war with the leg to see who would have the honor of bringing it to Junior. The bigger brother won and ran over to Junior's bed. He laid the leg on Junior's lap and sat on the side of the bed, jiggling up and down.

Junior didn't even feel the pain of having his legs bounced. On his lap was Ralphie's leg. Ralphie's leg!

"Big mouth," sneered Ralphie from the next bed. "When I get my new leg, the first thing I'm going to use it for is to kick your guts out."

Walking the Plank

✤   ✤   ✤

"HAND UP THE BOARD."

Vern was up in the crook of the elm tree by the jail. Maggie was below him, hiding a ten-foot board between her and the trunk of the tree.

"Someone's coming," she hissed.

"Look innocent," he hissed back.

"I am innocent!"

The man walked slower as he saw Maggie flattened against the tree. When she saw he was going to stop, her eyes got as round as cartoon eyes.

"Oh, hello." She pulled her lips up into a smile.

The man combed his hair with his hands. "Are you all right?"

"Of course."

"It's late, isn't it, for you to be out by yourself?"

"Yes, but my dad's a cop. He'll be out in a minute. He told me to wait here. I'm not supposed to go inside because children aren't allowed. My dad thinks criminals are a bad influence."

"Do you want me to go in and tell your dad you're out here?"

"He knows," Maggie said quickly. Behind her the board began falling forward, and she stopped it with her head. She looked up at the man through her eyelashes.

The man watched Maggie and the board for a full thirty seconds. Maggie shoved the board back against the tree with her head and stared right back at him.

Overhead, in the tree, Vern waited without breathing. Ever since he had gotten the idea of breaking into jail, he had been gripped by a kind of excitement he had never felt before. He was amazed that his ordinary, everyday mind had thought of it. Breaking *into* jail!

It had come to him in a flash. One moment he had been standing there with Maggie, looking stupidly at the jail, wondering what to do, and the next moment the idea burst out of his brain like one of those fantastic Dr. Seuss trees, too wild and wonderful to be real.

He gazed down through the leaves where the man stood with Maggie. He could see the man's bald spot. Vern took in a deep breath and closed his eyes in prayer.

Finally the man remembered when he and his gang used to steal lumber at night to build a clubhouse. With a smile, he shrugged and went on down the street.

Again Maggie got ready to pass the board up to Vern. "Here," she said. When she felt him take the board, she put her hands on the bottom and boosted it the rest of the way.

"I got it," Vern said. "Let go."

Maggie moved back into the shadows by the jail and watched. The only sound was the rustling of elm leaves as Vern and the board made their way up the tree. The rustling stopped across from the open vent of the jail.

Slowly the board appeared from the side of the tree.

Slowly it extended across the sidewalk. Slowly it waved up and down like one end of a seesaw.

"You're too low," Maggie called. "You're going to miss it by a mile."

The end of the board scraped against the side of the jail. It was about five feet below the vent. It rose shakily in the air. Then it wavered, trembled, turned sideways, and clattered down to the sidewalk.

"Verrrrn," Maggie said.

"I didn't do it on purpose," he snapped from inside the tree.

"Well, that could have hit me."

The only answer was the rustling of leaves as Vern made his way down.

Maggie got the board and dragged it back to the tree trunk. She waited for Vern's "Hand it up."

"Here."

"I got it."

"Be careful this time."

Maggie was glad she had gotten in the last word. She went back and stood in the shadows, this time far out of the way of the elm tree.

Again she heard the rustling of leaves, again she saw the board coming out like a gangplank.

"Too high," Maggie called.

Vern groaned and heaved and shoved, and by a miracle —that was how it seemed to Maggie—the board swept across the gap and landed on the ledge. It snapped into place as neatly as something from a Lego building set.

"Now," Maggie called, "all you have to do is walk across."

"That's all," Vern echoed.

Up in the tree he eyed the narrow board, and his heart sank. Vern had never admitted it, but he had always been aware that he did not have the daring his brother and sister had. Junior wanted to be a stuntman, Maggie wanted to be a trick rider, and he wanted to do something no one in the family had ever done—work in an office.

He dreamed of sharp pencils and unlimited stacks of paper and paper clips and rulers. His happiest moments in school came when the teacher asked them to fill out forms. That, he felt, was the closest he had ever come to office work. He handed in the neatest forms of anyone in his class.

That's why it was such a miracle that he had not only conceived this brilliant, ingenious plan but was putting it into effect.

He stepped on the board. He jiggled to make sure it was steady.

Maggie saw the shaking leaves and called, "Be careful. Don't fall, whatever you do."

Vern did not answer. He put his right foot in front of his left, heel to toe, then took one more step. He was holding on to the overhead branches, working on balance. He took another step. Another.

Then the branches stopped. Vern stood for a moment, holding the last two leaves, one in each hand. Then, with a sigh, he let go.

He held his arms out to the side. No circus tightrope walker had ever concentrated harder.

Vern kept his eyes on the vent. Heel to toe, toe to heel, he made his way across the board. His arms seesawed gently in the cool night air. He did not look down once.

Below, Maggie stood with her hands clasped. She appeared to be, and was, praying.

"We need Junior for this," she said.

"Thanks," Vern said through tight lips.

The board was beginning to sag. With every step it bent lower, buckling under his weight. Ahead he could see that the board was slipping closer to the end of the ledge. He took another heel-to-toe step.

The board sagged lower.

"Vern," Maggie called. "Did you notice that the board's starting to bend?"

Vern did not answer. He figured that one more step was all the board could take. One more step, and he and the board would crash to the pavement.

At that awful moment, with his arms waving at his sides, his heart pounding in his throat, the vent going in and out of focus before his tear-filled eyes, Vern made the decision of his life.

Vern jumped.

Traveling Mud

❧   ❧   ❧

MUD WAS MAKING HIS WAY THROUGH THE FINEST SEC-
tion of town, Maple Leaf Manor, where the rich people
lived. He loped along the smooth white sidewalks, taking
his time, pausing now and then to lift his leg on a wrought-
iron mailbox or a particularly fine piece of shrubbery.

An occasional car passed, lighting up his pale fur, giving
a red look to his golden eyes. Mud paid the cars no attention.

He slowed. His sharp ears had picked up the sound of
running water. It came from behind this house, and he
turned onto the soft manicured lawn. He ambled around
the house to the swimming pool, where a spray of water
ran continuously down the silver sliding board.

He stretched out on the cool tiles around the pool, stuck
his head over the side, and lapped the clear chlorinated
water. It wasn't as good as toilet water or creek water,
which he was accustomed to, but Mud was thirsty.

When he had drunk all he wanted, he spent a few seconds licking stray drops from his legs and feet. He chewed
a flea on his ankle.

Then Mud got to his feet. He stretched. He was getting ready to lift his leg in the direction of a lounge chair to mark the fact that he'd been there.

Suddenly, from the right, Mud heard a long, low *"Rrrrr-rrr."*

The hair rose on Mud's back. His sharp eyes looked in the shadows of a small walkway between the double garage and the house.

There Mud could see the high pointed ears of a Doberman. He could see the gleam of long white teeth.

The Doberman drew in enough breath to give another, longer *"Rrrrrrrrrrrrr."* An answering growl rose in Mud's throat.

The Doberman leapt forward, throwing himself at Mud. He choked on his chain and fell back. He tried to attack again.

Mud hesitated. Mud had never started a fight in his life, but Mud had never run from a fight either.

Now he was ready for battle. His teeth were bared. His hair was up. His eyes were bright. If the Doberman got free, Mud would meet him more than halfway.

The Doberman was barking wildly, throwing himself in Mud's direction, trying either to break his chain or to pull the whole house down. Between leaps the metal links rattled against the slate floor.

"Franklin!" a voice called from an upstairs window. "Be quiet down there."

"Maybe it's a burglar, Sam."

"All right, already. I'll take a look."

Mud stood still, frozen at the edge of the pool. The patio lights went on. Mud lowered his tail. He heard sounds at the door: the unsnapping of the dead-bolt lock, the click of the doorknob. Franklin was barking wildly, knowing his owner was on the way. He was facing the door now, legs stiff with anticipation.

As the door opened, Mud ran around the pool. He whipped through the hedge and galloped across the lawn like a racehorse.

Behind him a voice said kindly, "What's wrong, Franklin? You all right, boy?"

Franklin whined with pleasure.

"Was some stray dog after your bone?"

Mud hit the sidewalk and slowed. He lifted his leg on a bush at the Doberman's driveway, then he took the time to scratch the grass vigorously with his back feet. A spray of fine zoysia grass flew into the night air.

Then, without a backward glance, Mud ambled down the sidewalk, on his way to Pap.

The Missing Harmonica

JUNIOR COULD NOT GET TO SLEEP. THE LIGHTS IN HIS room had been turned out. The hospital hall was as quiet as it ever got. Ralphie had gone to sleep with the little harmonica in his mouth, and every time he breathed out, he played a soft, soothing chord. Still Junior could not sleep.

Usually the only time Junior had trouble sleeping was Christmas Eve. Even the times when his mother had the terrible Christmas Eve talks with them, warning in her quiet way that sometimes Santa couldn't bring everything everybody wanted.

Even when she looked directly at him during the terrible talk, and he knew, knew deep in his bones, that it was he who was not going to get the bicycle, he still could not sleep from excitement.

This was different. It was the opposite of excitement. They did a lot of opposites in school. The teacher would say, "The opposite of day is—"

"Night!" Junior would cry.

"The opposite of lost is—"

"Found!"

Junior had never missed a single one. Sometimes he was a little bit slower than the rest of the class, but he had never missed one.

This was impossible, though, he thought. He went over it again. "The opposite of excitement is—"

There was only one answer: "Lying in the hospital with hurt legs."

And his legs did hurt. They had not hurt much during the day, and they had stopped hurting entirely when he had held Ralphie's artificial leg and worked the knee. He had even for one brief moment wanted a leg exactly like the one on his lap.

Now, however, his legs were making up for lost time. They hurt a lot.

He realized suddenly how much he loved the sounds of his own house. He missed them. Mud drinking loudly out of the toilet, Pap grinding his teeth, the wind chimes they had given their mom for her birthday clicking musically on the porch below, the occasional chinaberry dropping on the tin roof.

He felt so miserable that he reached for the buzzer beside his pillow. "Use this, Junior, if you need anything," the nurse had told him, but he never had. Ralphie spent a lot of time ringing his buzzer, demanding Cokes and candy over the intercom as if he were the president of the hospital. When the nurses ignored him, he pressed the buzzer and made terrible gagging noises or pretended to be choking.

Now Junior looked at his buzzer. He pressed the button. A voice on the intercom said, "Yes?"

"It's me—Junior," he answered miserably.

"Speak up, please."

"It's me—Junior."

"What's wrong, Junior?"

"I don't feel good."

"Do your legs hurt?"

"Yes."

"I'll bring you an aspirin."

"Thank you," he said politely. It was hard not to be polite to a voice coming from the wall.

But when the nurse arrived with the paper cup and the pill, he was crying too hard to swallow. "I want Maggie," he wailed. "I want Pap. I want Vern. I want my mommmmmmmm!"

"Will you shut him up?" Ralphie said, flipping over in disgust. "Where does he think he is—at a hog-calling contest?"

The nurse wrapped her arms around Junior and hugged him. He tried to pretend they were his mom's arms, but it didn't work. Still, he was glad to have arms of any sort around him. "Tomorrow, you know what you're going to do?" the nurse asked kindly.

He shook his head against her.

"You're going to get up and sit in a wheelchair and you can go down to the TV room, and you can roll up and down the hall, and the play lady comes with games and books and you can pick anything you want."

"Is that true?" Junior asked.

"Big deal," Ralphie sneered.

"Go to sleep, Ralphie. You—"

Ralphie clutched his throat. "I swallowed my harmonica."

"Come on, Ralphie, it's too late at night for that kind of foolishness."

"I swallowed my harmonica, I tell you! I'm not kidding! I really swallowed my harmonica! Where is it if I didn't swallow it?"

He began to pull at his pajamas, frantically searching the wrinkles. He tore his pajama top open and shook it. He lifted his pillow.

The nurse crossed to Ralphie's bed. "Let's take a look. It probably fell down in your covers." She pulled them back and searched among the wrinkled sheets. "Roll over." She ran her hands under him.

"He did have it in his mouth," Junior said helpfully. "It blew a note every time he breathed out."

"Ralphie, it looks like you'd have better sense than to go to sleep with a harmonica in your mouth. If I have to send you down to X-ray, and there's no harmonica inside you, I'm going to be—" She shook the top sheet so hard, it billowed and snapped. "—furious."

"If you swallow a harmonica, do they have to cut you open to get it out?" Junior asked.

"Nobody's cutting me open!" The words burst from Ralphie. His hands folded into fists. "I'm not going to let anybody cut me open. The doctor promised me this was the last time I would have to—"

"There," the nurse said, "is your harmonica."

"Where?"

The nurse bent and picked something off the floor. She extended her hand. "There."

Ralphie looked at it suspiciously. "It doesn't look like my harmonica. How do you know it's mine?"

"Because nobody else on this floor has an inch-long

harmonica. Now, I'm putting this in my pocket, Ralphie, and you can have it when you leave the hospital."

"I don't want it anymore."

"I do," said Junior quickly.

"Take it," said Ralphie, turning away from them.

"All right, you can have it when you leave the hospital," the nurse said. "And do you want this pill or not?"

"I don't need it anymore," Junior said truthfully. The thought of owning his own harmonica was painkiller enough.

Before he went to sleep, Ralphie said, "I knew it was on the floor all the time. I just wanted to scare her."

"And you did," Junior answered.

Breaking In

PAP WAS NOT ASLEEP AND HE HEARD THE NOISE OF THE board thumping into place against the vent over his head. He dared not hope it was the children, and yet he could feel his heart begin to race in his chest.

He stood up. Pap had to stand up in stages. He stood up first in a stoop, and when his legs got used to that, he straightened the rest of the way up.

Now he stood tall beside his bunk, his head straining painfully toward the window, his old neck twisted like a rooster's. He heard nothing. With his head back, his Adam's apple stuck out as far as his sagging chin.

He said softly, "Kids?"

No answer.

"Kids?"

He wanted to whistle, but the man in the next cell had threatened to kill him if he whistled like—the man did not know birdcalls—like a nuthatch one more time. Pap wasn't afraid of the man, but he didn't want a disturbance of any kind just now.

He heard a new noise. He couldn't place it. A soft silk-smooth sound overhead. He held his breath. He waited. He knew in his bones that the sound had something to do with him.

Everybody else in the jail was asleep, snoring, snorting, groaning in their dreams. And they had gone to sleep instantly, because none of them were expecting anyone to drop in. Pap was, and so he alone waited alert in his lighted cell.

Even though he still couldn't place the thump, followed by the soft sliding sound, he knew it was his. His daddy used to have a saying long ago: "That piece of pie's got my name on it," and that was exactly the way Pap felt about the soft sliding noise overhead.

He waited with his hands twitching at his sides, his fingers making little beckoning movements.

The door opened, and a policeman came in for his hourly check. It was twelve o'clock.

The policeman walked slowly down the room, looking in each cell. He paused at Pap's cell. He looked Pap over from his shoes to his uncombed head. Pap's heart stopped beating.

"You better lie down, sir, get some sleep," the policeman said.

"I will. I will."

"You got a big day tomorrow."

"What?"

"Isn't your hearing tomorrow?"

"My what?"

"Your hearing."

"Oh, my hearing."

Pap nodded. He slumped to his bunk to get rid of the policeman. He lay down. He pretended to close his eyes.

Through a slit in his left eye he could see the policeman was still there.

He couldn't hear the soft sliding noises because the blood was pounding so hard in his head, it blocked out everything else.

"You a baseball fan?"

"What?" Pap's eyes snapped open. He was so filled with hope and dread and pounding blood, he couldn't even remember what baseball was. "Yes. No."

"Which is it?" The policeman smiled.

"Yes."

"Well, the Cards won. Braves won. Phillies lost."

"Oh."

Pap pulled back his lips in a smile. He swallowed so hard, his Adam's apple bobbed up to his chin.

Now at last, the policeman was moving back down the cells and into the office. The door closed.

With a sigh of relief Pap started to get to his feet. He was at the first, bent-knee stage, when he heard the noises outside.

There were three of them: a muffled scream, a soft thud against the side of the building, and then a long, loud clanging noise as something hit the sidewalk. It clattered, and then there was silence.

Pap scrambled onto his bunk.

"What's happened?" he called to the vent. "What's happened?"

He waited with his mouth open, like a thirsty man waiting for raindrops.

"What's happened? Please, somebody tell me what's happened!"

His feet were digging into his thin mattress, his hands

gripping the concrete wall. It looked exactly like he was climbing up the wall, except that he wasn't getting any higher.

"What's happened?"

There was a long pause. Minutes went by. Pap was so still, he could hear the ticking of his pocket watch. Then Pap saw the most beautiful sight of his life. A hand came through the vent and clutched the sill.

"Vern," he asked, still not daring to hope, "is that you?"

"It's me," Vern answered.

Maggie Alone

MAGGIE WAS STILL WAITING ON THE SIDEWALK, LOOK-ing up at the lighted vent with her mouth open.

If she lived to be a hundred, she would never forget Vern's desperate leap for the building. He had flung himself through the air, his arms and legs churning like an Olympic jumper's. Then he slammed into the wall, and his thin hands gripped the ledge. He had hung there for what seemed to Vern and Maggie to be the longest minute and a half in the history of recorded time.

Maggie kept waiting for him to fall to the ground. Vern kept hanging there.

Maggie glanced around. She wished she had something to put under him to break his fall.

When Maggie saw the board, she got a brainstorm, the first of her life. "Hold on," she yelled.

She took the fallen board, upended it, shoved it up against the wall, and gave Vern's dangling feet a boost. It was all Vern needed.

One foot found a toehold. His other knee pushed his body out from the wall. He worked the toe of his shoe between the bricks, and he pulled himself up six inches. His toe moved up a brick.

Vern inched his way up the rest of the wall, moving as carefully as a mountain climber, his tennis shoes digging into the wall, his hands reaching into the vent. It was a slow, superhuman, agonizing effort that Maggie watched from directly below.

She watched Vern wiggle eel-like through the vent. He had to turn his head sideways, the vent was so small, and she turned her head sideways too. She had sucked in her breath as he, too, had done to get his chest through the vent. She pulled in her stomach as he went over the sill.

For a few seconds there had been just his thin legs sticking out of the vent. Then they disappeared in a scissors kick, and Vern was in the city jail.

The leap had been so exciting, and her part in it so spectacular, that Maggie had wanted to jump up and down and cheer. It had been like something out of the circus, the most exciting, successful moment of her entire life.

Now, however, with the realization that Vern was inside with Pap and that she was outside with nobody, all she felt was lonely.

"Vern!" she called softly.

It had been ten minutes since Vern's legs had disappeared.

"Vern?"

Tears came to her eyes and spilled onto her cheeks. Usually when Maggie cried, she wiped her tears away with the ends of her braids. It was the best part of having braids. That and crossing them under her nose and making a mustache. Those were the only two reasons she went to all the trouble of making the braids. Now she was too miserable to care.

"Vern?"

Far above her, in the light of the vent, Vern's small, round face appeared. Maggie lifted her arms like a mother urging her child to jump.

Vern said just one sentence before he slipped back into the jail and out of sight.

"Junior's in Alderson General Hospital."

In the jail Vern tumbled once again into Pap's trembling arms, and the two of them sat down on the side of Pap's bunk. The first few minutes of the reunion had been spent with Pap rubbing his hands over Vern, testing to make sure he was real, mumbling, "I knew you'd come. I knew you wouldn't let me down."

The next minutes were spent realizing that now, instead of having one family member in jail, they had two. After that, they hadn't said anything, just sat enjoying the comfort of each other's presence.

Finally Vern had broken the silence with "Maggie's outside."

"That's what I figured," Pap said.

Pap knew it wouldn't be proper to bring a girl into the men's half of city jail. Then, with a sudden lift of heart, he remembered Junior.

Junior had been worrying Pap ever since the policeman had told him Junior was in the hospital. Now the heavy lines between Pap's brows eased. Things were working out all right after all. Maggie could take care of Junior.

"I'll boost you up, and you yell out and tell her Junior's in Alderson General Hospital."

"That's all?"

"She'll know what to do."

Vern had climbed on Pap's old sloping shoulders, turned his head sideways, poked it through the vent, and looked down at Maggie's pale face far below.

He called, "Junior's in Alderson General Hospital." Then he shinnied down Pap's body as if it were a tree, and joined him on the bunk.

No one in the jail had awakened.

Pap, comforted at last, leaned back against the concrete block wall. Vern did too. Their eyes closed.

Vern opened his eyes. "I forgot something. Boost me up again, Pap."

"Verrrrrrrrrn," Maggie wailed. She stood with her head back like a howling dog. "What am I supposed to do nowwwwwww?"

She looked down at the board at her feet. Maybe she could get it up the tree and across the gap to the ledge so Vern could come back across. She knew she couldn't. It had taken all her strength to lift it up for that one short boost. Maybe she could do something terrible and get arrested. "Just put me in with my family," she would tell the arresting officer, "—the Blossoms." She would look so pitiful that—

At that moment, with tears of pity welling in her eyes, Maggie heard the clink of a coin at her feet. She brushed her tears away with her braids.

The clink was followed by another. Then money

poured from the vent. It fell around her like rain—nickels, dimes, pennies, wadded-up dollar bills.

Even before the last coin hit the sidewalk, Maggie was on her hands and knees, gathering it in.

Rich and Special

MAGGIE FELT BETTER. IT WAS SURPRISING HOW MUCH more wonderful things looked when you were rich.

The money was in her jeans pocket—nineteen dollars and forty-nine cents. She had wrapped it up like a package, securely, with the dollar bills folded around the coins.

"Isn't it late for you to be out by yourself?" the bus driver asked.

Maggie was sitting on the long sideways seat behind him. Now that she had money, everything seemed to be going her way.

The bus had stopped. She had said, "By any chance do you go past Alderson Hospital?"

The bus driver had said, "I sure do."

She said, "How much?"

He said, "Fifty."

She said, "Just a minute." She unwrapped her package of money, dropped the money in the slot, and here she was, on her way.

Life sure was easy when you had money.

"I asked," the bus driver said again, "isn't it late for you to be out by yourself?"

"Yes," she admitted, "it is."

"You got family in the hospital?"

"My little brother."

"What's wrong with him? Is he hurt, sick, or what?"

"Hurt, I think."

The bus driver steered the bus around a corner, and Maggie leaned with the turn. She was the only passenger on the bus.

"Where's the rest of your family?"

"Well, my other brother and my grandfather are in city jail."

"In jail? You're putting me on."

"I wish I was."

"In *jail?*"

"Yes, it's true."

"What'd they do?"

"I don't know exactly what Pap did. Vern went in on his own, through the vent."

"Your brother busted into jail?"

"That's right. I helped him."

"*Into* jail? Now you are jiving me."

"No, I'm not."

"And you helped him?"

"I gave him a boost."

"Man, this don't happen. People don't bust *into* jail. Who-all knows he's in there?"

"Just Pap."

"The police don't know?"

"Nope."

"Whoeee, they'll have themselves a nice surprise in the morning. Be the first time anybody ever busted into jail. I know some people like to bust out."

"Me too," said Maggie, thinking of Pap and Vern.

"Bust *into* jail—that just don't happen. Whoa, bus. Look, I'm 'bout to go past your stop. There's Alderson General."

Maggie looked out the window at the four-story building. "Well, I thank you."

"You take care of yourself. You the only member of your family doing all right. Everybody else in jail, in the hospital."

"I will."

Maggie felt rich and special. She decided it was a great combination. She got up and, holding her hand over the comforting wad of money in her pocket, got off the bus.

Junior was having the most wonderful, elegant dream of his life. He was in an orchestra, a huge orchestra, and he and all of the other musicians had on expensive black suits. The black suits were so expensive, they shone. They all—even the ladies—had on neckties.

In their hands were miniature silver musical instruments that really played. The instruments were the most beautiful things Junior had ever seen in his life.

The cymbals were the size of dimes. The piano was so small, the piano player had to poke the keys with toothpicks. The violins were one inch long; the bass fiddles, two inches. The orchestra leader had a baton like a straight pin.

Junior, of course, had his harmonica. He was in the front row. He was standing up. He had his music on a silver stand. A spotlight shone on him.

He was wiping his harmonica daintily on the lapel of his

black suit, getting the spit off for the second number, when a voice said, "Junior."

Junior did not open his eyes.

The orchestra leader was tapping his straight pin on his music stand. He lifted it in the air.

"Junior!"

The dream was too wonderful to lose. This was his one chance to be a star, to play in a real orchestra with chandeliers glowing and his black suit shining. This was the only time thousands of people in evening outfits would be smiling, waiting to clap for him. This was—

"Junior! It's me! Maggie!"

Junior opened his eyes.

Discoveries

❧   ❧   ❧

THE POLICEMAN WHO DID THE ONE O'CLOCK CHECK OF the city jail did not spot Vern. Vern was lying on the far side of Pap, against the wall, under the blanket, asleep. The two o'clock policeman didn't see him either; neither did the three and four o'clock policemen.

For three and a half hours Vern slept so soundly, he did not move one single time. Pap slept the same way. They might as well have been logs.

At four-thirty Vern moved for the first time. He slung one foot out from under the blanket and it landed on Pap's arm. Pap never even felt it.

The five o'clock policeman came in eating a ham and fried egg sandwich. He had been on duty all night and he was tired.

He just gave a quick check of the cells on the left, taking in with one glance the fact that everybody was in his bunk asleep. He turned his head, did the same quick sweep on the right.

He was ready to go back to the desk when he noticed something weird in the last cell. What in the— Take a look at that!

The old man's foot was on his arm. How did he manage that?

The policeman walked closer, his ham and fried egg sandwich forgotten in his hand. The only explanation he could think of was that the old man was some sort of contortionist, like the Living Pretzel whom the policeman had once seen in a sideshow.

But wait! What in the— Would you take a look at that!

There was a leg attached to the foot. It was a small leg. Too small.

The officer had been a member of the police force for twenty years but he had never seen anything like this. He walked closer. He saw now that the leg went under the blanket where there was a large bump. Coming out of the top of the bump was a lot of rumpled sandy-colored hair.

The officer unlocked the cell without making a sound. He entered. He pulled back the blanket so carefully, the sleepers never even felt it. He looked at Vern. He looked up at the open vent.

He closed his eyes, shook his head, and a half smile came over his face. *Well, we've had a jailbreak,* he said to himself. He laid the blanket gently back over the sleeping boy.

He went to the sergeant's desk. He shook his head. "You ain't going to believe this," he said.

Mud was hungry, and it was the first time in his life he had ever had to worry about food. His diet had always been simple. Whatever Pap ate, he ate. If Pap ate pancakes with syrup on them, he ate pancakes with syrup on them. If Pap ate stew, he ate stew.

Mud was moving into the downtown section of the city

95

now, and the houses were close together. There were no nice lawns, no side yards. There weren't any swimming pools or fine shrubbery either.

At one of the houses Mud paused. He smelled something of interest—a fishy smell. He lifted his nose, trying to find out where the smell was coming from.

Mud was fond of fish. Sometimes when Pap caught a fish in the creek, he would put it in a bucket of creek water and let Mud recatch it.

It was like bobbing for apples. Mud would thrust his whole head into the water, scramble around till he felt the fish in his mouth. Then he would come up.

Pap's laugh was Mud's reward, that and a piece of fried fish later. Mud held these fish in his mouth so gently, there was never a tooth mark on them.

Mud crossed the street. The smell seemed to be coming from this house . . . from this porch. Mud went up the steps. From this dish on this railing. Mud stood up and looked into the dish.

Mud was a good stander. He could even take a few steps on his hind legs when it was necessary. Mostly he stood up so he could get a better look at something.

It worked. Mud could see that the dish contained a ring of dark food, sort of smashed down into the bottom. He propped one foot on the banister and took the dish in his teeth. He set it down on the floor without a sound.

Mud took one small bite of the fish stuff. The taste was nothing like Pap's fish, and he stood looking at the dish with his brow drawn into wrinkles. He took a second bite.

This was the worst food Mud had ever had in his entire life. It was barely edible. If he hadn't been absolutely starved . . .

Mud finished the cat food, went down the steps, and was once again on his way through the dark streets of Alderson.

Ralphie opened his eyes and saw Maggie sitting cross-legged on the foot of Junior's bed. Her green eyes were shining; one of her braids lay on her tanned shoulder, she was chewing on the other in her excitement. Her cheeks were pink. She was grinning. She had one jagged tooth.

Even if she had not been telling the story of how she and Vern had busted into jail, Ralphie would have fallen in love with her. His heart was pumping hard, like the machines he'd seen occasionally through the doors of Intensive Care.

"You busted into jail?" Ralphie asked. He worked his way up in bed until he was sitting. He hadn't even bothered to push the control and bring the head of the bed up with him.

Maggie had learned from the bus driver the shock value of her story. Already it was her favorite story in the world. She loved to tell it. Her eyes got brighter.

"It was the only thing we could do. We had to."

"They had to," Junior echoed in the same delighted voice. He held out his empty hands to show there was no alternative.

"Pardon me for being nosy," Ralphie said, "but why didn't you just go in the police station and ask to see your grandfather?"

Maggie looked at him as if he were crazy. He wished he hadn't spoken. The tips of his ears turned red.

"Anybody could have done that," she said.

"Yes, anybody," piped Junior happily.

"We Blossoms," Maggie said proudly, "have never been just 'anybody.'"

Ralphie believed her. For the first time in his life he had nothing to say.

Fame

BOY BREAKS INTO CITY JAIL WAS THE HEADLINE. THE story took up two columns on the front page.

BULLETIN:

Last night a local juvenile broke into city jail by way of an old air vent. Using a board, which he placed in an elm tree beside the jail, he crossed to the vent. The size of the vent was approximately seven inches by fourteen inches.

According to police, the boy entered city jail just before midnight and slept in the cell with his grandfather, Alexander "Pap" Blossom, Sr., who is in jail awaiting a hearing on a charge of maliciously disturbing the peace.

Officer Canfield, the policeman who found the boy during his five o'clock rounds, admitted that it had been quite a surprise. "I knew soon as I saw him that he wasn't supposed to be there. I went out and got the sergeant and took him in, and the sergeant was surprised too. He shook both the boy and the grandfather awake to find out what was going on."

When awakened, the grandfather asked one question, "What's wrong?" The officer admitted that the boy was still in his grandfather's cell but would be moved, he said, "as soon as we figure out what to do with him."

"We let him out for breakfast, but he wanted to go right back in afterward, so we let him. We're taking it one hour at a time."

The grandfather's hearing is scheduled for this afternoon.

There was a large picture of Pap and Vern sitting on the bunk, side by side. Their hands were on their knees, their heads turned stiffly to the photographer. It was like a photograph taken fifty years ago.

Neither one of them looked scared, unhappy, or regretful.

Under the picture was the caption: "Local policemen caught off-guard by unique jailbreak."

"Hey, you weren't kidding!" Ralphie said.

Ralphie had been walking up and down the hall on his new leg, mainly in the hope of impressing Maggie. At the desk he had seen the morning newspaper.

"I want to borrow this," he said.

He hurried back to the room, hopping spryly on his new leg. "There." He threw the paper, headline up, on Junior's bed.

"That's them!" Junior cried, drawing in his breath. "They're famous!"

"Give me that," Maggie said.

"What does it say?"

"This is what it says." Maggie snapped the newspaper open. She read the story aloud, stumbling only on the words *juvenile* and *maliciously.* When she was through, she held the paper at arm's length and looked at the picture critically.

Then she said, "That doesn't look a thing like Vern, does it, Junior?"

"Not a thing." Junior was so glad to have Maggie with him that he had become her echo.

"And they made Pap look like an old bum."

"A real old bum," Junior said.

Ralphie said, "Reporters try to take unflattering pictures. That's part of their training. They throw the good pictures in the trash can."

For the first time Maggie looked at him with interest.

"He tells lies," Junior said quickly, seeing Maggie's look. He did not want to share Maggie with anybody. "He told me he had watermelon seeds inside him and marbles in his head."

Ralphie's ears turned red.

"Maybe he lied about that," Maggie admitted. She was beginning to like the boy with the artificial leg. "But he sure tells the truth about reporters."

"Maybe," Junior conceded.

Ralphie was so pleased with Maggie's compliment that he hopped around the room on his artificial leg.

"Stop that, Ralphie!" the nurse called from the door. "You're supposed to walk on the leg, not jump on it. You're going to bust those stitches."

"It doesn't hurt at all," Ralphie said, lying.

Trucks and Cabs and I-85

MUD DID NOT KNOW WHAT TO DO ABOUT THE INTER-
state. The only time he had been on I-85 before, he had
been sitting beside Pap in the cab of the pickup, with
wind that smelled of exhaust fumes whipping his ears
back from his face.

He had come to I-85 today at the peak of the midday
traffic. He had turned down the exit ramp because the air
in that direction smelled more familiar than the air in any
other direction. Now he faced more traffic than he had
ever seen in his life.

He waited and watched. He knew he had to get across it
—the air told him that—but he didn't know how. The
traffic was solid—a double line of trucks and cars and
buses and vans, all exceeding the speed limit.

He walked nervously back and forth, pacing, his eyes on
the steady stream of traffic coming through the under-
pass. He breathed air thick with exhaust fumes. He
blinked every time a truck threw gravel in his direction.

Mud's tongue was hanging out. His throat was dry. He
had not had a drop of water for three hours, not since the

cat-food snack. And the cat-food snack had left him thirsty.

An hour ago he had come across a dust hole. With Mud, there was nothing to do with a dust hole but get in it and roll around. Mud preferred the back method. He lay on his back and twisted from side to side. His eyes closed in bliss, he moaned with pleasure.

Afterward, refreshed, he got up and shook himself. A red cloud grew around him.

As he left the dust hole he felt better but looked worse. To see him loping along the side of the road, a person would think Mud had never had a bath in his life. The bandanna around his neck looked like a dust rag.

A small break came in the right lane. Mud started out, then darted back as a truck roared down the fast lane at seventy-five miles an hour. Mud crouched on the grass while fine gravel rained around him. He fell back to wait for another chance.

He was going to get across I-85 if it killed him.

"Well, I better be on my way," Maggie said with studied casualness.

Maggie had been in the hospital for twelve hours, and she could not have been happier if she had been in the ritziest hotel in New York City. Everything she wanted, or would ever want, was right here.

She had just finished lunch. She had bought a pimento cheese sandwich from a vending machine, heated it miraculously in a small oven, and washed it down with an ice-cold Mello-Yello.

Before that she had napped in the waiting room, on a long plastic sofa, while watching *Let's Make a Deal.* She got to see a man dressed like a hot dog win a Westinghouse refrigerator. This was living.

"Be on your way?" This was the worst news Ralphie had ever heard in his life. He was at her side in an instant. "Where are you going?"

Maggie yawned. "To the courthouse, of course. My grandfather's hearing is this afternoon."

"You're going to the hearing?" Junior wailed.

Junior was in a wheelchair for the first time, his legs propped in front of him. He rolled himself forward a few inches. "I want to go too."

"You can't."

"I have to!"

"No."

"I *have* to!"

Junior could not bear to be left again. He had not even started to recover from being left on the roof. That was the worst thing that had happened to him, worse even than the broken legs. Breaking legs he could stand; being left he couldn't.

"I'm sorry, Junior, I would never be able to get you on the bus," Maggie said sensibly. "I rode the bus last night and there was not one single wheelchair person on it. There are no ramps, no—"

"You can get me on. Please! I promise you can get me on," Junior wailed.

"Junior, you have two broken legs. You're in a wheel-chair!"

"I'll walk if you get me crutches. I promise I'll walk. Please!" He would have gone down on his knees if he had been able to bend.

"No."

"Then I'll get my own crutches."

Junior propelled himself toward the door, but this was his first time in the wheelchair. The chair swerved into the foot of his bed.

Junior hung his head in defeat. He began to cry. "I want to go! I want to go!"

Maggie was softened by his tears. "I'll tell you all about it when I get back. I'll remember every single thing that happens. It'll be just like being there."

Junior shook his head from side to side in a fit of rage and frustration too terrible to be expressed in any other way. "No! No! No! No—"

It was Ralphie who stopped the explosion of *no*'s. He took one step forward on his artificial leg.

"We," he said. There was something in his quiet, take-charge voice that made Junior stop crying and look up. "We could take a cab," Ralphie said.

Maggie looked at him and her face lit up with Junior's. At that moment they looked like brother and sister.

Maggie threw her braids behind her back and grinned, showing her jagged tooth. "Why didn't I think of that?" she said. "Of course! We'll take a cab."

Going to Court

"Gentleman to see you," the policeman told Pap.

Pap threw up his hands to protect himself. "No more reporters. I'm not talking to no more reporters." His old head wagged tiredly from side to side, begging for mercy.

"Me either," said Vern who was sitting beside him.

"This is not a reporter. It's a lawyer."

Pap's head snapped up. "Lawyer?"

"The best the town's got—Henry Ward Bowman."

"What's he want with me?"

"He says he wants to defend you."

"For how much?" Pap asked suspiciously.

"For free."

Now Pap was even more suspicious. "Why?"

"You want my opinion?"

Pap nodded reluctantly. He hated to ask a policeman for anything.

"Mr. Bowman's getting ready to make a run for the state senate, and I imagine he thinks it wouldn't do him any harm to get you off and get himself some publicity doing it. You may not know this, but we've had more calls about you and the boy than about anything else that's ever happened in the police department, even the Safeway robbery last year. People don't like to see a grandfather being arrested for nothing more than defending a load of pop cans from some reckless teenagers. People don't like to see a boy forced to bust into jail to be with him."

Pap watched the policeman with sharp eyes, taking in every word.

The policeman shrugged. "That's how the public sees this whole thing anyway."

That was how Pap saw it too. He started stage one of getting to his feet—the crouch. Then he rose to his full height of six feet.

He tucked his shirttail into his pants. He fished in his hip pocket for a comb. He raked it through his tangled hair, then he swept the sides back like wings, the way he did on special occasions.

He slapped the comb against his palm to clear it of stray hairs. Then he slid it back in his pocket.

"Show Mr. Bowman in," he said.

It was two o'clock in the afternoon, and Mud had started barking at the traffic. He had been trying to cross I-85 for thirty-five minutes, and the traffic wouldn't let him.

Mud was tired, sore of foot, thirsty, and desperate. Most of all, he wanted Pap.

At two-ten someone threw a can out of a car window. It struck the concrete beside Mud and bounced into his side. Startled, Mud shied away, almost backing into traffic coming down the ramp.

It seemed to Mud then that he was surrounded by danger. There was no safety anywhere. In a panic he headed for the interstate.

The right lane was clear. A semi was barreling down the fast lane.

Ears back, tail down, Mud ran.

"I'll do that," Ralphie said. He took Junior's wheelchair, unlocked two springs underneath, folded it in half, and snapped it shut with practiced skill.

Junior was in the backseat of the yellow cab with his legs resting on Maggie's lap. Ralphie put the folded wheelchair in the front seat and squeezed in beside it.

"Courthouse, please," he told the driver.

The driver nodded, and the cab moved out from under the hospital awning.

"Good-bye, Hospital," Junior called with a happy wave.

The cab made the turn onto Main Street. It began to pick up speed.

Maggie spent the first few minutes of the cab ride admiring Ralphie. For those few minutes she watched the back of his shaggy head and returned his love wholeheartedly.

Ralphie was a man of the world, the first Maggie had known. She remembered with admiration the quick, assured way he had maneuvered them out of the hospital. It had been like something out of a movie.

"Hold the elevator, please," he had called. Someone held it.

Ralphie swirled Junior's chair around and guided it in the elevator backward. "Thank you," he said in the same tone of voice Maggie heard hospital workers use. "Every-one going to the lobby?" he asked, pushing the L button.

The nurse at the desk yelled, "Where are you taking Junior, Ralphie?"

"Gift shop," Ralphie called back cheerfully as the doors began to close.

"Bring him back this—"

The word was cut off, but inside the elevator Ralphie supplied it with a smile: "—instant."

Everyone on the elevator laughed, and they were swept down to the lobby. It was like a miracle. Maggie kept taking sidewise glances at Ralphie. He kept his eyes on the elevator doors.

"Coming through," Ralphie called as they came off the elevator. People in the lobby made way for them.

"Cab!"

And the cab pulled up in front of the hospital. It was as if the cab had been waiting just for them. This was the way things went for celebrities, Maggie thought: instant ser-vice.

"Courthouse, please." Ralphie said it as if he went daily to the courthouse.

Maggie sighed with pleasure. She was beginning to ap-preciate people who knew how to handle themselves in this increasingly complex world.

She leaned back and admired the way the city of Alder-son looked through the window of a yellow cab.

Order in the Court

❧ ❧ ❧

THE STORY OF VERN'S JAILBREAK WAS PICKED UP BY every newspaper in the country, and the picture of Vern and Pap was on every front page, including the front page of *The Pecos Daily News and World Report* of Pecos, Texas.

Vicki Blossom was coming out of the TexiMex Motel with two girlfriends she was sharing a room with. Another friend was waiting for them. This friend was leaning against the fender of the pickup truck they were driving to the rodeo; she was reading the newspaper.

"Hey, Vicki," she called, folding the newspaper against her so the front page was hidden, "isn't Pap Blossom your daddy-in-law?"

"Yes."

"Does he still live in—" She opened the paper and checked the name of the town. "—Alderson?"

"Last I heard," Vicki said cheerfully. She was swinging her hat in the air.

"And have you got a little boy about ten or eleven?"

"Vern's eleven, Junior's seven." She stopped swinging her hat.

111

"Have you talked to them lately?"

"The lady at the motel said Vern called about four days ago—this was when we were at the Paisano—but the only message was that everything at home was all right. I didn't get to talk to him because I was sharing a room with you guys and my name wasn't on the register." She came forward with her hat in both hands. "Why?"

When her friend was slow in answering, Vicki said again, sharply this time, "Why?"

"Because according to this newspaper everything is not so all right."

"What? Let me see. Gimme."

Vicki Blossom took the newspaper with hands that had started to tremble. "Oh, my Lord," she said, "look at that. My daddy-in-law and my oldest boy are in jail."

She started back into the TexiMex Motel reading the little print. "Go on without me," she told her friends. "I'm going home."

The courtroom was packed. Twelve reporters from state newspapers and representatives from NBC, CBS, and ABC were there with cameras. Both David Hartley and Bryant Gumbel had expressed an interest in interviews.

There were also 347 interested citizens who were trying to get into the courtroom for the hearing. Some of them had been interviewed by the reporters, and they all agreed that Pap should go free.

Pap, Mr. Bowman, Vern, and the two cardplayers who were defending drunk and disorderly charges sat on the front row. Pap had on a clean shirt and pressed pants which the lawyer had furnished him. Vern's hair had been wet and combed down flat. They both looked honest, respectable, and miserable. They couldn't wait to get out of court and look like themselves again.

The judge rapped his gavel.

The room got quiet. The bailiff announced that the Blossom case would be heard first. "Yes, there seems to be an unusual amount of interest in this matter," the judge said.

Pap got up in a stoop, rose, and followed his lawyer to the table. "You may be seated." They sat.

The judge told the lawyer prosecuting the case to begin. "I'd first like to call Officer Mahon," he said.

Officer Mahon was sworn in and the prosecutor asked him to describe what occurred on the afternoon Pap was arrested.

"Well, sir, we got a call about three-thirty Monday afternoon to go to Spring Street. The call came in from a citizen who reported a man with a gun had threatened some pedestrians. Also that the street was unusable, being completely clogged with beer and pop cans."

"What did you do after you got this information?"

"We went to the scene."

"And what did you observe?"

"We observed Mr. Blossom there on Spring Street with a weapon."

"Did you determine what kind of weapon it was and whether or not it was loaded?"

"Yes, sir. It was a single barrel shotgun and I could tell by the temperature of the barrel and the powder marks near the hammer that it had been recently discharged. From the evidence at the scene and based on my past

113

experience, I could tell that a traffic light had been hit by a shotgun discharge."

"After you made these observations what did you do?"

"I arrested Mr. Blossom."

"What was his attitude at the time of his arrest?"

"Mr. Blossom appeared confused as to the reason for his arrest. He did not think he had done anything wrong. We put cuffs on him and got him into the patrol car. After that, he never said a word or gave us any trouble."

"Thank you, Officer Mahon."

Mud was on the median strip of I-85. He had managed to cross the southbound double lane, and now faced the northbound. He had intended to run straight across both of them, but there had been some nice pine trees planted in the median strip, and Mud was so exhausted he lay down under the low branches.

He closed his eyes. A flea crawled in the dusty fur behind his ear. He was too tired to scratch. The steady drone of traffic seemed far away.

Without opening his eyes he settled his body into a more comfortable spot in the pine needles and fell asleep.

Mr. Bowman was on his feet. He was an inch taller than Abraham Lincoln, and he had the same kind of old-timey eyeglasses. He looked around the courtroom over the top of them.

The judge said, "Mr. Bowman, it's a little unusual to see you taking an interest in this county's criminal court."

"I know, your honor, but my interest in justice is not limited to civil matters."

"Well, we're pleased to have you in court today. You may proceed."

"Thank you, your honor. I'd like to begin by calling Pap Blossom."

Pap got up in a stoop, rose, and took the stand.

The Rest of the Blossoms

THE YELLOW CAB PULLED UP IN FRONT OF THE COURT-house. In the backseat Maggie had taken out her package of money and was unwrapping it carefully, preparing to count out the $4.65 cab fare.

"I'll get it," Ralphie said casually, as if he paid for cabs every day of his life.

"Why, thank you." Maggie folded up her money.

"It's nothing," Ralphie said. Then he surprised himself by adding something he had heard only on television: "Keep the change."

Actually he was extremely relieved that he had had enough money. If his mother had not left him five dollars to pay for his TV rental, he wouldn't have.

Ralphie got out of the cab and skillfully unfolded the wheelchair. Maggie and the cabdriver helped Junior get in.

Junior was so excited over going to court and being in a wheelchair that he couldn't stop grinning. He kept closing his lips over his teeth because he knew it wouldn't be proper to grin in criminal court, but he couldn't help himself. He didn't want to grin, but his lips did.

He glanced at Maggie to see if she was giving him a disapproving look. It made him feel a little better to see that Maggie was smiling too.

"Let me push him up the ramp for you," the cabdriver said.

"Thanks," Ralphie said quickly.

Now that the money crisis was over, Ralphie had started worrying that he wouldn't be able to push Junior up the ramp without asking for help. His own leg hurt so bad, he wouldn't have minded having a wheelchair himself.

"Be careful with him," Maggie said.

"Don't worry. I was in a wheelchair myself for a year after the war."

A reporter who had arrived too late to get into the crowded courtroom was sitting on the courthouse steps. He watched their slow progress up the ramp. There had to be a story in these people.

The reporter got up. He said hopefully, "Do you three have anything to do with the man who got arrested and the boy that broke into jail?"

"We sure do," Maggie said. "The boy is our brother, and the man is our grandfather."

The man took their picture twice. He already had his caption: "Blossom family arrives at the courthouse."

"Wait, let me help you inside. I'll take them the rest of the way," he told the cabdriver.

They went through the double doors and made their way down the hall. The doors to the courtroom had been left open so that the overflow crowd could hear the case.

"Could we get through, please," the reporter asked. "This is the rest of the Blossom family."

Ralphie did not bother to mention he was just a friend.

117

He was honored to have been mistaken for a Blossom. He crowded through behind the wheelchair.

It was four o'clock and Mud awoke. He was rested. He lay for a moment without moving, his bright golden eyes watching the traffic below him on I-85.

He got up. He discovered with pleasure that the lowest limb of the pine tree was just over the part of his back that always itched. He moved back and forth, back and forth, scratching the spot on the convenient pine limb. He closed his eyes, blocking out the traffic and the noise in the pleasure of scratching the spot that only he and Pap knew about.

Pap was always good about scratching Mud with his shoe. Mud would see Pap's foot dangling at just the right height, and he would go over and stand under it. Pap never failed to move his foot exactly where it itched.

The pine limb was a good substitute, though. The loose bark rained around him.

When Mud's itch was satisfied, he moved out from under the pine tree. The traffic had thinned, but Mud wasn't thinking about that. Mud had just smelled water, and Mud was very thirsty.

He moved to the right, nose up. The smell seemed to be this way. He went over the slight hill that bulldozers had created between the highways. The grass was soft and had just been mowed.

Mud skirted another stand of pine trees. The smell of water was stronger. He turned his nose down like a divining rod.

In a deep grassy ditch a small stream of water trickled

into a drainage pipe. Mud's eyes shone, and he bounded down the slope.

He drank lustily, his rough tongue brushing against the corrugated pipe. He had never tasted better water in his life, not even from the family toilet.

He drank, and when that little puddle of water was gone, he moved deeper into the pipe. Another small pool of water between those ridges. Mud drank. He moved deeper into the pipe, drinking between each ridge, enjoying it more because it was cool and scarce.

Mud moved through the pipe in a stoop, drinking as he went. There was not a sound of the traffic overhead until he came out the other side. Then he heard it—the cars and trucks behind him.

The air smelled familiar this way, so he ran up the embankment. There was a chain-link fence there, blocking his way. Mud didn't hesitate. Mud knew what to do about fences.

Mud began to dig.

The Verdict

Maggie, Ralphie, and Junior got through the crowd at the back of the courtroom. The first thing they saw was Pap walking back to the table with his head down. His face was as red as a beet.

Pap was in misery. His head was pounding. His throat was dry. He took out his worn handkerchief and wiped the sweat from his face. His hands were trembling.

It wasn't the fear of going to jail that was making him miserable. He'd been in jail and it wasn't so bad. It wasn't the fact that he could be fined five hundred dollars. A man couldn't pay what he didn't have.

It was being questioned. Pap had never been able to abide people asking him questions. Nobody in his family could. It was a family trait.

And here he had to sit as if he were in chains, and let anybody ask him anything they wanted to—the prosecutor, the judge, and Henry Ward Bowman, who was trying to act like Lincoln.

A dozen times he had wanted to interrupt and say, "Just send me to jail and get it over with." It would have been a relief to be led back to his corner cell.

The only thing that stopped him was that out of the corner of his eye he could see Vern's feet, Vern's worn tennis shoes. Above all, Pap didn't want to make Vern's jailbreak seem like it had been in vain.

"In conclusion, your honor," Mr. Bowman was saying, "Mr. Blossom has had an absolutely clean record. He has a high and respected reputation in this community. He has never been arrested; he has never gotten a traffic ticket; and it is only through the series of unusual and bewildering events which he testified about this afternoon that we are even here today. Mr. Blossom is not a criminal and he should not be found guilty of a criminal offense."

Pap was so lost in misery that the judge had to rap his gavel on the desk three times to get his attention.

"Mr. Blossom!"

Pap looked up.

"I said I have reached a decision in your case."

The lawyer helped Pap to his feet.

"Mr. Blossom, I agree with your lawyer that the events of Monday were to a large extent the result of a chain of unfortunate incidents. However, it is my duty to protect the lives of the people of this county. We cannot allow citizens to take the law into their own hands."

Pap nodded.

"I find you guilty on the charge of disturbing the peace and sentence you to sixty days in county jail."

Pap nodded. He turned and headed for the door, where the policeman waited to take him back to his cell.

"However—"

The lawyer stopped Pap and turned him around.

"However, because of the circumstances and because you obviously have the wholehearted love of at least one member of your family," the judge nodded at Vern, "I am suspending your sentence on the condition that I do not see you in this court again."

Pap nodded.

"Mr. Blossom, you may go now."

Pap stood blinking in the courtroom. He spoke willingly for the first time since he had entered the courtroom. "Home?" he asked in a bewildered, incredulous way.

"Yes, Mr. Blossom, you are free to go home."

Mud was a good digger. He never dug around the farm unless it was a gopher or snake hole and Pap indicated it was all right to dig. Pap would do this by pointing with the toe of one worn shoe at the hole. "What's that, Mud?" Pap would ask. "What's down there?"

Mud would dive in. He would dig so hard the dirt would fly over his back. He never actually got his teeth on a gopher or snake, but he sure was a good digger.

It took Mud seventeen minutes to dig the hole halfway under the fence. Then he had to dig the rest of the way on his side, working his lean body under the chain, pushing the dirt behind him with his paws.

He squirmed out on the other side and immediately began shaking the clay from his fur. He still felt dirty. There was a patch of grass by the trees and Mud rolled in that. Then he shook himself again.

Satisfied, he started through the woods.

Maggie cried, "Pap!"

She pushed Junior down the aisle and to the front of the courthouse so fast, Junior screamed. He thought his legs were going to ram all the way through the judge's desk. The judge rapped his gavel.

"It's us!" she cried.

In bewilderment Pap watched her come. Maggie let go of the wheelchair to throw her arms around him, then around the startled Vern. She had never embraced either one of them before.

Junior's chair did a wheelie which left him facing the room and the reporters. Cameras clicked.

The judge rapped again for order.

"Perhaps," the judge said, "the Blossom family could continue this family reunion in my chambers."

"That's very kind, your honor," the lawyer said. As the cameras rolled, he ushered them all toward the chamber door, imagining how fine this would look on the evening news.

At the door Maggie turned and beckoned to Ralphie. "This includes you," she said.

Going Home

❧ ❧ ❧

RALPHIE AND JUNIOR WERE ON THEIR WAY BACK TO THE hospital in a police car. Neither one of them had put up a fuss. They were glad to go. Both of them wanted to get back in bed. Their legs hurt.

"I'll come see you," Maggie had said to Junior. She leaned down and looked into the car so she could see Ralphie too. "I'll come see both of you."

She grinned, showing her chipped tooth, and threw her braids behind her shoulders. Then she closed the car door.

"Good-bye," Junior said. Then, after a pause, he added, "Maggie," so she would know he was speaking to her instead of the courthouse.

For the first time in his life he was not saying good-bye to a building, even though this afternoon the courthouse had become Junior's all-time favorite building in the world. He really loved the courthouse. He loved his family more.

"Good-bye, Pap!" He called through the glass. "Good-bye, Vern!"

Vern and Pap didn't hear him. They were on the steps

of the courthouse having their pictures taken. Both Pap and Vern would have been long gone except that the lawyer had an arm around each of them and was bodily holding them in place. Their arms were clamped straight down at their sides.

Reporters were calling out questions as if it were a news conference. Vern's questions were: "Son, tell us how you decided to break into city jail? How did you feel when you got inside? Were you scared? Would you do it again? Have you got anything to say about security at city jail?"

Pap's questions were: "Sir, how did you feel when you saw your grandson coming through the vent? What are your plans now that you're free? What did the boy's mother say when she heard he was in jail? Do you ever plan to collect any more pop cans?"

Neither Pap nor Vern said a word. The lawyer did the talking. Finally, when he'd had all the attention he was likely to get, he lifted his hands. Pap and Vern started down the steps. The reporters followed.

"Now, you guys give these folks a break. They've been through a lot. I'll tell you exactly what we're going to do. First we're going to ride over and get Mr. Blossom's truck, and then he and his grandchildren are going home. I am too."

With a laugh, Henry Ward Bowman guided Pap and Vern to his car. He got in the front. Vern and Pap and Maggie squeezed in the back. Mr. Bowman and Maggie waved for the cameras. Vern and Pap did not.

It was dusk and Mud stopped to lick his foot. It hurt. His tongue found a sharp point that wasn't supposed to be there. Something had stuck into his foot, between the pads, a thorn of some kind.

Mud tried to take the stub in his teeth. It was too short. He dug into the flesh of his foot so deeply, his nose wrinkled. It hurt a lot, but this time he got the end of the thorn.

Mud pulled it out and spit it on the ground. He looked at it closely before he went back to licking his sore paw.

Mud was so intent on his sore paw that he failed to hear a noise behind him. He kept licking.

A skunk stuck his head out of the hollow tree behind Mud. The skunk couldn't see Mud because of the ferns. Mud hadn't seen the skunk for the same reason, and Mud had not smelled the skunk because the skunk was downwind.

The skunk was beginning his evening search for food. It was beetle and bug season, and they were all fat, crisp, and oily. Next month there would be crickets and grasshoppers and, after that, caterpillars. The skunk was hungry.

The skunk came through the ferns, as he always did. His nose was to the ground. His tail was relaxed.

Mud got up. Now he heard the noise behind him. Ferns rustled; parted. He swirled around. The hair rose on his back.

Too late he saw the long pointed nose, the black and white fur. Too late he recognized the smell.

Mud's tail dropped between his legs at the same moment that the skunk swirled, flared, thumped his hind legs on the ground, and sent a stream of liquid in Mud's direction.

In an instant Mud was blinded. He ran yelping with pain and fear around the small clearing. He ran into trees and briars, senselessly trying to run away from the pain and the fear and the blindness, and getting nowhere.

Skirting the yelping, panic-stricken dog, the skunk proceeded on his evening rounds. He found a beetle under the first stone he overturned.

"Drop me off at the emergency entrance," Ralphie told the policeman as they turned into the hospital.

"Me too," Junior said. If he could help it, he would never be separated from Ralphie again.

Ralphie turned to him. "We can pick up another wheelchair for me and a couple of interns and get pushed up to our room."

"Good," Junior said.

"We'll probably be there in time for supper."

"Good." Suddenly Junior had his first unpleasant thought of the afternoon. "Maybe," he said in a rush, "they really will put medicine in our food now. Maybe because we ran away, they'll want us to be so groggy we can't do it again."

"Nah," said Ralphie. "They wouldn't dare."

Mud's Missing

"WHERE'S MY DOG?"

"What?"

"The dog that was in the truck. Where's my dog?"

This was the first time Pap had ever worried about Mud. He never had to before because Mud was the most sensible member of the Blossom family. He knew what he was supposed to do, and he did it. It was as simple as that.

Pap had not doubted for a minute that Mud would be with the truck, in the back, curled up on his gunnysack. Either that or he would be nearby getting something to eat or drink.

When he saw the man's blank look, he let out a piercing whistle that went up and down like a siren. It could be heard for a mile.

"I don't know anything about any dog," the man at the garage said, stepping back out of Pap's reach.

"Who towed Mr. Blossom's truck in?" the lawyer asked.

"When was this?"

"Monday."

"Pete was working Monday, I believe. Arnie, ask Pete if he knows anything about this man's dog."

The Blossoms waited in silence by the truck. Maggie had gotten so used to things getting better that tears of disappointment filled her eyes. It had seemed like the whole rest of her life was going to be like that—better and better and better. Now, after just one day of getting better, it was getting worse again.

And she had not given one single thought to Mud! She whisked the tears away with the tips of her braids.

Pete came out of the garage wiping oil off his hands. "I never seen any dog," he said.

"He was a tall dog," Vern said, "with gold-colored eyes and a red bandanna around his neck. His name was Mud."

"I never seen a dog of any description."

Pap touched one finger to his forehead, trying to remember whether Mud had gotten out of the truck at the scene of the accident. If he had, Mud most likely would be there, on Spring Street, waiting. He gave another whistle just in case.

"You could put an ad in the paper," Mr. Bowman said. "Or, better still, let the newspaper do a story for you. Your family is news now, Mr. Blossom. Call the paper and tell them about your dog—what was his name?"

"Mud."

"I'll call them for you and ask them to send a reporter to the farm. Somebody in town will have seen the dog."

The Blossoms kept standing around. None of them wanted to leave, because it would be like giving up on Mud.

Pete said helpfully, "Your truck's running good. We tuned her up and took care of the expired inspection sticker. Mr. Bowman took care of the license. You're ready to roll."

Still the Blossoms stood there.

Finally Vern said, "Pap, maybe we ought to go. Maybe Mud's waiting downtown."

"That's what I'm hoping," Pap said.

He led the way to the truck and they got in. "You folks have a nice day," Pete called after them.

Ralphie's mother was waiting for Ralphie in the hospital room. The minute she saw him she leapt up from her chair. She had come to the hospital in such a rush that she had on a dress over her bathing suit.

Ralphie said, "Hi, Mom. What are you doing here?"

Ralphie's mom said, "Don't you 'hi' me, and I'll tell you exactly what I'm doing here."

Ralphie's mom said, "Ralphie, the nurse called me on the phone and told me what you did. I cannot believe that you would take this little boy with two broken legs in a cab to the courthouse. Do you realize that you could have done permanent injury to this little boy? The nurse said today was the first time he had even gotten up. One of his legs is broken in two places. If you have done any damage to either one of that little boy's legs, your dad's going to wear you out."

Ralphie's mom turned to Junior. "Are you all right? I am just so sorry for what my son did. I apologize for him."

"He didn't do me any damage," Junior said. "I enjoyed it."

Pap hated to return to the scene of the accident. As soon as he turned the corner onto Spring Street, it all came back to him—the abrupt stop, the falling cans, the boys in the Toyota, the police attack.

132

"Right here's where it happened," he told Vern and Maggie in a low, sad voice.

There was a parking slot in front of Woolco, and Pap backed into it.

The three of them got out. Pap let out a piercing whistle. Everybody on the block turned around to find out where the noise had come from, but Mud did not come bounding into view with his ears flying, eyes shining, as they had hoped.

"Maybe he's around back," Vern said, "where they throw the garbage. Maybe he's back there eating out of the dumpster."

"Go see."

Maggie and Pap waited, without speaking, for Vern to come back. Their hope died as they heard him calling "Mud! Mu-ud! Mud!" from the back of the Winn Dixie.

Vern came around the store shaking his head.

"Not there?"

"No."

"Well," Pap said. "That's that." He sighed so deeply that he seemed to get shorter. "Well, there's nothing to do but go home."

"There's still the reporters," Maggie said. "I know they'll be able to find him. I *know* they will."

"Maybe," Pap said. He swallowed, almost choking on his next words because he hated reporters so much. "If they do, I'll be mighty grateful."

The three of them climbed into the truck. As they drove off, Maggie said, "You look on that side of the road, Vern, and I'll look on this side. Maybe we'll see him."

They watched all the way home, but neither of them did.

133

In the News

✢   ✢   ✢

A DESCRIPTION OF MUD APPEARED IN THE STATE PAPER along with a story about the trial. The headline was BLOSSOM DOG LOST FOLLOWING OWNER'S ARREST.

BULLETIN:

Yesterday, following the release of Pap Blossom, it was learned that his dog, Mud, had been frightened during his owner's arrest and had run away. Several people reported seeing a dog fitting Mud's description running through the downtown area.

Later Mud was spotted at a local Dairy Queen, lying beneath the carryout window. He appeared to be in a coma, one woman said. Several people offered him bits of food, but he would not eat. When the Dairy Queen opened the next day, the dog was gone.

The dog has not been seen since, although there have been various unconfirmed reports of a dog seen on I-85 yesterday afternoon.

Mud is a large dog with short, yellowish fur. He has golden eyes. He has a piece of an old red bandanna tied around his neck.

Anyone seeing a dog answering this description is asked to call the police department. Mr. Henry Ward Bowman, Pap Blossom's lawyer, has offered a fifty-dollar reward.

Beside the story, in the center column, was a police artist's composite drawing of Mud. Mud had never had his picture taken, so this was the best they could do.

Vern, Maggie, and Pap had been satisfied with the likeness.

"That's him," Pap said.

"Yes, that's exactly the way he looks," Maggie had said, "when he's feeling—" Tears filled her eyes. "—when he's feeling happy."

Vicki Blossom stopped for a hamburger at a diner just across the state line. She saw Mud's face looking at her through the newspaper dispenser. She got out a quarter as quickly as she could.

She went into the diner reading.

"Well, what next?" she asked the man on the stool next to hers. She showed him the front page. "My daddy-in-law was arrested, my little boy busted into jail to get him out, and now there's an all-points bulletin for our dog."

"I hear the old man got off."

She nodded. "That's what they tell me. I've been calling the police and the hospital and the lawyer. I can't get anybody. I'll be home this afternoon to see things for myself."

She ordered a hamburger and settled down to read the story.

"Look," she said, "there's all my kids. My youngest boy is in the wheelchair, two broken legs, and he's grinning like it's Christmas.

"There's Maggie, my girl, and she's got better sense than to take her little brother out of the hospital. She practically kidnapped him, according to the nurse. I don't know who this boy is. That's probably the cabdriver."

She looked close at the third picture. "This—I almost didn't recognize him with his hair combed—is my daddy-in-law, and this is my oldest boy, Vern. This man between them is the lawyer."

She drank some coffee to get the strength to look at the newspaper some more. She shook her head.

"I can't believe this. My whole family smeared across the front page of the state paper. I'm going to have to straighten every one of them out."

Ralphie said, "Well, good-bye."

"I wish you didn't have to go."

"I do, though. You heard my mom."

Junior nodded.

"You and everybody else in the hospital," Ralphie added.

Ralphie's mom had come to take him home that morning. She was still mad. She said, "If you can get around that good, good enough to tramp downtown to the courthouse, you can get around good enough to go home."

"I've got to have my therapy!" Ralphie had cried. "You want me to be a cripple?"

136

She pointed at him. "You"—it was like something Junior had seen once on a poster—"are going home."

"Well, can I at least put my leg on?"

She was already storming down the hall. She did not answer.

"You want me to read the story about Mud one more time before I go?"

Junior nodded. This would make the eighth time, but Junior would never get tired of hearing it.

" 'Bulletin: Yesterday, following the release of Pap Blossom . . .' "

The Hero

THE SIGHT OF HIS MOM IN THE HOSPITAL DOORWAY caused Junior to burst into tears.

She rushed to his bed. "Junior, let me look at you. I have been so worried. Darling, how are you?"

"I'm fine."

"No, you aren't. Let me see those legs." She threw back the sheet. "Both of them. You broke both of them." Tears came to her eyes too.

He nodded.

"Well, one good thing about our family is that our bones heal fast. Your dad broke seventeen bones in his lifetime and never spent one day in the hospital. He took the casts off himself."

Junior's mom always knew how to make him feel better. He wiped his tears on the sleeve of his pajamas. "Did they find Mud?"

The newspaper was still on his lap. He had shed so many tears on the composite drawing of Mud that the picture looked bubbly. Since Ralphie had gone, Junior had not had anyone to read the story to him, but he had looked at the pictures so much, he had them memorized.

138

The cheerful one of himself in his wheelchair was his favorite. He would feel better every time he looked at that one. Then he would see Mud, and tears would drop from his eyes. He was careful not to get any on his own picture.

"I don't know, Junior. I haven't been home. I drove straight to the hospital to see you. Sandy Boy's outside in his trailer."

"I went to the courthouse."

"I know you did. I read about it in the newspaper."

"The boy that was in that bed took me, but he's gone home."

"Well, you'll be going home, too, now that I'm here to take care of you. I'm going right down and talk to the nurse."

"Talk to the big redheaded one," Junior called after her. "She's the nicest."

His mother disappeared around the door and started down the hall. There was a pause and then Junior sat straight up in bed.

"Get my harmonica!" he yelled.

"I keep hearing something. Do you?" Maggie said. "It sounds like Mud, but he's real far away."

"You *think* you hear something."

"No, I do."

"You *wish* you heard something." Vern corrected her because he wanted her to know he understood exactly how she felt. He had been hearing things himself. "Maybe it's thunder."

Maggie nodded. "Maybe." She dropped down beside him on the steps. "Mom's coming home this afternoon."

"I know it. I was standing right beside you when the policeman told us."

"I wish she'd hurry."

Maggie stretched out her legs. As usual she had on boy's clothes. She was older than Vern but smaller, so she got what he had outgrown. Today she had on a pair of his last summer's shorts and a shirt so old, it didn't have a button on it. Maggie had tied a knot in the shirttails to keep it closed.

After a long moment Maggie said, "You know, Vern, it wasn't a stupid idea after all."

"What?"

"Your idea. Busting into jail."

Vern had come to that conclusion himself, but it was something he longed to hear about. "Why do you say that?" He shifted his feet and looked at Maggie out of the corners of his eyes.

"Well, because if you hadn't busted into jail, Pap wouldn't have gotten off, and Mom wouldn't have seen the newspaper, and she wouldn't be coming home. Why, if you hadn't busted into jail, we'd be right back where we were that night outside the jail—desperate and helpless."

Vern swallowed. He closed his eyes as if the world had suddenly gotten too bright to look at. He was speechless with pleasure.

"Vern," she said, and then she added the most beautiful sentence Vern had ever heard, one he would never forget: "You are a hero."

Family Favorites

VICKI BLOSSOM WAS FIXING BREAKFAST. SHE WAS FIXING the family favorite: fried shredded wheat. She softened the shredded wheat in hot milk, and then she put it on the griddle, flattened it with the spatula, and fried it. The Blossoms ate it with lots of syrup.

"Anybody want seconds?" she asked. When nobody answered, she looked around. She couldn't believe it. "Nobody?"

The three kids shook their heads.

"Well, all right. I'll save these for Pap."

At the moment Pap was off looking for Mud. All day yesterday and at dawn today he'd been in his pickup truck, riding around town, whistling out the window for Mud.

"You're just wasting gas, Pap," Vicki had told him.

"Not if I find him," Pap answered. "It ain't wasted if I find him."

"Well, at least wait until the rain lets up."

"I can whistle for him in the rain good as I can in the sunshine."

141

And he had driven off, whistling. The rain coming in the window poured down his wrinkled face.

"All we need is for you to catch pneumonia!" she called after him.

Vicki watched her children at the table. "Are you kids still moping about that ugly dog?" She shook her spatula at them.

The Blossom kids looked down at their plates to keep from meeting her eyes.

"I'm ashamed of you kids. Count your blessings. Pap's out of jail. Junior's out of the hospital. I'm home, and you're moping about Mud. If you can't live without a dog, go to the pound this afternoon and get another one."

"Mom!" Maggie looked up in shock. "That's a terrible thing to suggest."

"We could get a puppy," Junior said. He liked the idea. "A puppy is not a dog."

"It is, too, Junior," Maggie said. "Anyway, it's not our dog, Mom; it's Pap's. Mud lets us play with him, but he's Pap's dog. That's why I feel bad. Pap really loves Mud."

"Pap is old enough to hide his feelings. If he wouldn't go around with that long, sad face, looking like he'd lost his best friend, whistling out the truck window like a lunatic, you wouldn't feel bad. Shoot, I felt bad leaving the rodeo. The rodeo's in my blood—you know that. But I didn't mope around, making everybody else feel bad too. Pap needs to grow up."

She slapped a flattened shredded wheat on her plate. It was one of the ones she had been saving for Pap. She sat at the table and ate it angrily, without syrup, cutting it up so hard with her fork that pieces shot off the plate.

142

Mud was rolling in a patch of wet Bermuda grass. He nosed his way through, rubbing his stinging eyes against the cool grass. He had spent the past eight hours rolling in whatever he could find—moss, leaves, dirt, mud, a small stream, a bank of ferns. None of it got rid of the smell.

His eyes still felt scratchy, but at least he could see now. After the spray hit his face, his eyes had watered so much and so long that a lot of the irritation had been washed away.

He twisted over and rubbed the other side of his face. Then he got up and shook himself. He saw a stand of pine trees, and he went over and rubbed his face against the rough bark. Turning, he did the other side.

It was nice under the pines. The branches shielded him from the rain. Like Pap, Mud had never cared much for rain.

He lay down and rolled in the pine needles, nosing them from side to side, still trying to get the scent off his face.

He rested a moment. Mud was exhausted. He had not had a real meal in four days. His ribs showed through his fur.

Still, there was something comforting about lying under these particular pine trees. He had lain here before. Maggie had pushed him under here one hot summer afternoon and said, "Now you're the wolf and I'm Hiawatha. You stay under there until I come by and I don't see you and I don't know you're there. Pretend like you're going to eat me."

He had waited on the soft bed of needles—waited, without understanding why, for the okay to come out. With the memory growing sharper, urging him on, Mud squirmed out from under the branches. He stood for a moment, smelling the air.

Then he began to bark wildly as he bounded through the woods. He leapt over bushes, logs, the creek. He charged down the ravine, up the other side. His shrill barks rang through the woods and echoed. The sound was continuous, like the ringing of bells on a joyous occasion.

Together

"SEE IF YOU CAN GUESS WHAT THIS SONG IS," JUNIOR said. He put his harmonica in his mouth. He kept it on a string around his neck because of Ralphie's unfortunate experience. At least if he swallowed his harmonica, he could pull it back up.

"I'm tired of guessing," Maggie said. "Let Vern guess this one."

"They all sound the same to me," Vern said.

"No, this one's different."

Junior began to play.

Vicki Blossom was at the sink, washing the breakfast dishes. She had just opened the window, and she was the first to hear Mud's wild barking.

"Well, you kids can stop moping," she said over her shoulder. "I hear Mud."

She opened the back door and went out on the stoop, drying her hands. Maggie and Vern ran out too. Junior was desperately trying to maneuver his wheelchair around the kitchen furniture.

"Wait for me! I want to see too!"

Mud came out of the trees like a streak; he tore up the incline where the Blossoms threw the garbage; he leapt over the old tractor. He headed for the house.

Vicki threw back her head. "Oh, Lord, he's been skunked. Get back in the house. Quick." She held her nose. "Get back, Maggie. Close the screen door. Quick! Junior, get out of the way." She spun his wheelchair around. "Close the door, Vern. Close it!" She reached around and slammed the door herself just as Mud hit the porch.

Mud leapt up and down, throwing himself at the door. His happy face appeared framed in the high glass pane every time he jumped.

When she had watched his face come into view seven or eight times, Maggie said, "I don't care. I'm going out."

She turned the knob and slipped through the door. "Me too," Vern said.

"Well, you're not coming back in this house, either one of you, if I catch one whiff of skunk on you or your clothing."

"We know."

Maggie and Vern threw their arms around Mud.

"Well, they can split us up," Pap said. He was in the creek, washing Mud with heavy-duty detergent. "But we Blossoms always manage to get back together. That's the good thing about being a Blossom."

"One of the good things," Maggie said.

This was Mud's seventh bath. For the first two or three he had spent a lot of time trying to get out or shake the soap off, but now he was resigned to being washed.

He stood without moving. His ears were flat against his

146

head. His tail was between his legs. His eyes rolled occasionally up to Pap.

"I hate it as bad as you do," Pap told him.

Maggie and Vern sat on the bank, watching. Maggie had on another old outfit of Vern's, and her braids were still wet. "Tomorrow," her mom had told her, "I'll make you a French braid. I learned how to do it in a beauty parlor in Pecos. Hey, maybe I'll go to work in a beauty parlor. That always was my second love."

Vern's hair was wet, too, combed with a part. "You kids have got to start fixing yourselves up," their mom told them. "Maggie, I'm getting you some dresses."

"And cowboy boots."

"We'll see."

"Okay, Mud, that's probably about as good as we're going to do." Pap rinsed him off with a bucketful of water. Mud closed his eyes as Pap poured another bucket over his head.

"Go roll in the grass," Pap told him. As soon as Mud heard the word *go* he went.

He leapt up the bank and shook himself. Drops of water hit Maggie and Vern, and they turned their faces out of the way. Mud rolled in the grass. He got up, shook himself, rolled again.

Pap stepped out of the creek with the aid of a small tree. Pap used trees like walking sticks. He pulled himself up the bank.

He said, "Vern, I noticed a lot of beer and pop cans when I was riding into town. After lunch, what say we go pick them up?"

"Fine with me," Vern said.

148

"Well." Pap straightened. "Let's go up to the house and see if we smell good enough to be allowed inside."

And with Mud leading the way, the Blossoms headed for home.

About the Author

BETSY BYARS's sharp perceptions and skill at penetrating the inner life of children have made her one of America's most popular and honored writers for young people. In 1970 her *Summer of the Swans* won the Newbery Award, and her first book for Delacorte Press, *The Night Swimmers,* won the American Book Award for juvenile fiction in 1980. Ms. Byars is a licensed pilot and lives in Clemson, South Carolina.